TREASURY OF FAIRY TALES

FOREWORD BY NAOMI LEWIS

BARNES
&NOBLE
BOOKS
NEW YORK

Contents

When Dreams Came True

FAIRY TALES FOR THE YOUNG

Long Ago and Far Away
FAIRY TALES FOR OLDER CHILDREN

Foreword

THERE IS A COUNTRY where you are always welcome, especially if you are any age between two and ten. Every time you arrive, many good friends wait to greet you and take you where you wish. One of the best things about this Otherland is that no one need know you are there. You don't even have to move. You will seem to be in school, in bed, at the dinner table, anywhere usual. "Dreaming again?" someone might say. But mostly no one will notice.

"How do I get there?" you might ask. Easily. A direct way lies in this book. Each story that you will read will take you further into the Otherland. When you have read them all, you will have an invisible pass for a lifetime. It's worth having, I can tell you. You'll be surprised how often you are likely to use it. Remember – listen and read carefully – the magic is in the words.

And who are those waiting friends? Well, besides Red Riding Hood, Hansel and Gretel, and other such regulars, there will be elves who do your chores by night, various talking birds and beasts (a cunningly helpful cat among them), mermaids, a witch or two, plenty of friendly princes and princesses, sometimes even the Snow Queen herself. Take care to be polite to certain wise old women. They know all the secrets and are ready to work some useful magic at your need. Good manners are never forgotten in Otherland. (This holds for the "real" world, too.)

Fantastic journeys abound throughout these stories. Children accustomed to the ranging wildness of nursery rhymes will not quail at joining the heady voyages in Otherland. For the youngest, I recommend the cheerfully crazy farmyard march of Henny-Penny and friends. For older explorers, there is Kay's sleigh ride with the Snow Queen, high in the vast, dark wintry sky.

"They rose up high, and she flew with him over the dark clouds, while the storm-wind whistled and raved, making him think of ballads of olden time. Over forest and lake they flew, over sea and land; beneath them screamed the icy blast; the wolves howled, the snow glittered; the black crows soared across the plains, cawing as they went. But high over all shone the great clear silver moon."

And from *The Wild Swans* comes another memorable skypiece: Elisa's swan-borne flight towards the elusive cloud palace of the fairy Morgana, which no mortal may enter.

> "As she gazed, mountains, palace, trees and flowers all dissolved … All she saw was a whirl of mist over the water. Sea and air and sky are ever in motion, ever changing; no vision comes to the watcher twice."

The rewards aren't easily won in these tales, or there would be no story. But they are won at last, and splendidly. *The Ugly Duckling* is an example. Are you laughed at, misunderstood, the one never chosen at games? This tale is yours. Are you searching for something – or someone – lost? Nothing in fairy tales can match Gerda's quest for the lost Kay in *The Snow Queen*.

I think it is worth considering why genuine fairy tales never become out-of-date, unfashionable. It is because they have at their core certain unchanging truths; their images still hold, years after the first childhood meeting. To a rational adult almost all of the happenings in even the simplest of these tales are stranger than anything they are ever likely to know. For young children, though, Otherland life, the life of story, has just as much reality as that of the daily human round. When I say today, Will I ever find a way through this forest of thorns? Will the pieces of ice ever come together?, anyone with a child's pass to Otherland will assure me that the answer will eventually be Yes.

Start reading now!

NAOMI LEWIS

Once Upon a Time

Goldilocks and the Three Bears

TRADITIONAL ~ RETOLD BY ANN MACLEOD AND
ILLUSTRATED BY WENDY SMITH

ONCE UPON A TIME there were three bears who lived together in a pretty little cottage in the middle of a wood. There was a Little Tiny Wee Bear, a Middle-Sized Bear, and a Great Big Huge Bear. Now these bears were very fond of porridge and they each had their own porridge bowl: a little bowl for the Little Tiny Wee Bear, a middle-sized bowl for the Middle-Sized Bear and a big bowl for the Great Big Huge Bear. And they each had a chair to sit on: a little chair for the Little Tiny Wee Bear, a middle-sized chair for the Middle-Sized Bear and a big chair for the Great Big Huge Bear. And they each had a bed to sleep in: a little bed for the Little Tiny Wee Bear, a middle-sized bed for the Middle-Sized Bear and a big bed for the Great Big Huge Bear.

One fine summer morning when the Middle-Sized Bear had made the porridge and poured it into the three porridge bowls, the three bears decided to go for a walk in the wood while the porridge cooled, for they did not like burning their tongues by eating the porridge when it was too hot. So away they went through the wood — the Middle-Sized Bear and the Great Big Huge Bear walking along slowly while the Little Tiny Wee Bear ran in front and turned somersaults because it was such a beautiful morning.

While the three bears were out walking a little girl called Goldilocks came running through the wood. She stopped in surprise when she saw

the pretty little cottage and she stood on tiptoe and peered in the window. Seeing nobody inside, she turned the door handle. The door opened and in walked Goldilocks.

Now Goldilocks was not a very nice little girl or she would never have walked into another person's house without being invited. And now, when she saw the porridge on the table, she felt hungry and decided to have some herself, which again was not a very nice thing to do.

First she tasted the porridge in the big bowl but that was too salty for her. Then she tasted the porridge in the middle-sized bowl but that was too sweet for her. And then she tasted the porridge in the little bowl and that was just right, and Goldilocks liked it so much that she ate it all up.

Then Goldilocks sat down in the big chair and that was too hard for her. Then she sat down in the middle-sized chair and that was too soft for her. And then she sat down in the little chair and that was just right. But she sat herself down with such a bump that the bottom came out of the chair and Goldilocks fell through on to the floor.

Then Goldilocks went upstairs to the bedroom where the three bears slept. First she lay down on the big bed but that was too high at the head for her. Then she lay down on the middle-sized bed but that was too high at the foot for her. And then she lay down on the little bed and that was just right. So Goldilocks covered herself up with blankets and lay there comfortably until she fell fast asleep.

Soon the three bears came home to breakfast, and the first thing they saw was the three spoons standing in the three porridge bowls.

"Someone's been eating my porridge," said the Great Big Huge Bear in his great rough gruff voice.

"Someone's been eating my porridge," said the Middle-Sized Bear in her middle-sized voice.

"Someone's been eating my porridge and has eaten it all up!" squeaked the Little Tiny Wee Bear in his little tiny wee voice.

The three Bears began to look around the room.

"Someone's been sitting in my chair," said the Great Big Huge Bear in his great rough gruff voice.

"Someone's been sitting in my chair," said the Middle-Sized Bear in her middle-sized voice.

"Someone's been sitting in my chair and has broken the bottom out of it!" squeaked the Little Tiny Wee Bear in his little tiny wee voice, and he burst into tears.

The Middle-Sized Bear put a cushion across the broken seat and gave the Little Tiny Wee Bear some of her porridge so he stopped crying, and when the Great Big Huge Bear had made sure that there was nobody hiding in the kitchen the three bears went upstairs to their bedroom.

"Someone's been lying on my bed," said the Great Big Huge Bear in his great rough gruff voice.

"Someone's been lying on my bed too," said the Middle-Sized Bear in her middle-sized voice.

"Someone's been lying on my bed and she's still there!" squeaked the Little Tiny Wee Bear in his little tiny wee voice.

Goldilocks had heard in her sleep the rough gruff voice of the Great Big Huge Bear and the middle-sized voice of the Middle-Sized Bear, but only as if she had heard someone speaking in a dream. When she heard the little tiny wee voice of the Little Tiny Wee Bear it was so sharp and shrill that it wakened her at once. When she saw the three bears standing at one side of the bed she tumbled out of the other side and jumped out of the window. Then she ran away through the wood as fast as she could, and the three bears never saw her again.

Henny-Penny

TRADITIONAL ~ RETOLD BY JOSEPH JACOBS AND
ILLUSTRATED BY NICHOLAS ALLAN

ONE DAY HENNY-PENNY was picking up corn in the cornyard when – whack! – something hit her upon her head. "Goodness gracious me!" said Henny-Penny. "The sky's a-going to fall; I must go and tell the King."

So she went along and she went along, and she went along till she met Cocky-Locky. "Where are you going, Henny-Penny?" said Cocky-Locky.

"Oh! I'm going to tell the King the sky's a-falling," said Henny-Penny.

"May I come with you?" said Cocky-Locky.

"Certainly," said Henny-Penny. So Henny-Penny and Cocky-Locky went to tell the King the sky was a-falling.

They went along, and they went along, and they went along till they met Ducky-Daddles. "Where are you going to, Henny-Penny and Cocky-Locky?" said Ducky-Daddles.

"Oh! We're going to tell the King the sky's a-falling," said Henny-Penny and Cocky-Locky.

"May I come with you?" said Ducky-Daddles.

"Certainly," said Henny-Penny and Cocky-Locky. So Henny-Penny, Cocky-Locky and Ducky-Daddles went to tell the King the sky was a-falling.

So they went along, and they went along, and they went along, till they met Goosey-Poosey. "Where are you going to, Henny-Penny, Cocky-Locky and Ducky-Daddles?" said Goosey-Poosey.

"Oh! We're going to tell the King the sky's a-falling," said Henny-Penny and Cocky-Locky and Ducky-Daddles.

"May I come with you?" said Goosey-Poosey.

"Certainly," said Henny-Penny, Cocky-Locky and Ducky-Daddles. So Henny-Penny, Cocky-Locky, Ducky-Daddles and Goosey-Poosey went to tell the King the sky was a-falling.

So they went along, and they went along, and they went along, till they met Turkey-Lurkey. "Where are you going, Henny-Penny, Cocky-Locky, Ducky-Daddles and Goosey-Poosey?" said Turkey-Lurkey.

"Oh! We're going to tell the King the sky's a-falling," said Henny-Penny, Cocky-Locky, Ducky-Daddles and Goosey-Poosey.

"May I come with you, Henny-Penny, Cocky-Locky, Ducky-Daddles and Goosey-Poosey?" said Turkey-Lurkey.

"Oh, certainly, Turkey-Lurkey," said Henny-Penny, Cocky-Locky, Ducky-Daddles and Goosey-Poosey. So Henny-Penny, Cocky-Locky, Ducky-Daddles, Goosey-Poosey and Turkey-Lurkey all went to tell the King the sky was a-falling.

So they went along, and they went along, and they went along, and they went along, till they met Foxy-Woxy; and Foxy-Woxy said to Henny-Penny, Cocky-Locky, Ducky-Daddles, Goosey-Poosey and Turkey-Lurkey, "Where are you going, Henny-Penny, Cocky-Locky, Ducky-Daddles, Goosey-Poosey and Turkey-Lurkey?"

And Henny-Penny, Cocky-Locky, Ducky-Daddles, Goosey-Poosey and Turkey-Lurkey said to Foxy-Woxy: "We're going to tell the King the sky's a-falling."

"Oh! But this is not the way to the King, Henny-Penny, Cocky-Locky, Ducky-Daddles, Goosey-Poosey and Turkey-Lurkey," said Foxy-Woxy. "I know the proper way; shall I show it to you?"

"Oh, certainly, Foxy-Woxy," said Henny-Penny, Cocky-Locky, Ducky-Daddles, Goosey-Poosey and Turkey-Lurkey. So Henny-Penny, Cocky-Locky, Ducky-Daddles, Goosey-Poosey, Turkey-Lurkey and Foxy-Woxy all went to tell the King the sky was a-falling.

So they went along, and they went along, and they went along, till they came to a narrow and dark hole. Now this was the door of Foxy-Woxy's cave. But Foxy-Woxy said to Henny-Penny, Cocky-Locky, Ducky-Daddles, Goosey-Poosey and Turkey-Lurkey: "This is the short way to the King's palace; you'll soon get there if you follow me. I will go first and you come after, Henny-Penny, Cocky-Locky, Ducky-Daddles, Goosey-Poosey and Turkey-Lurkey."

"Why of course, certainly, without doubt, why not?" said Henny-Penny, Cocky-Locky, Ducky-Daddles, Goosey-Poosey and Turkey-Lurkey.

So Foxy-Woxy went into his cave, and he didn't go very far, but turned round to wait for Henny-Penny, Cocky-Locky, Ducky-Daddles, Goosey-Poosey and Turkey-Lurkey. At last Turkey-Lurkey went through the dark hole into the cave. She hadn't got far when "Hrumph!" Foxy-Woxy

caught Turkey-Lurkey and threw her over his left shoulder. Then Goosey-Poosey went in, and "Hrumph!" Goosey-Poosey was thrown beside Turkey-Lurkey. Then Ducky-Daddles waddled down, and "Hrumph!" Foxy-Woxy chased and caught Ducky-Daddles and threw him alongside Turkey-Lurkey and Goosey-Poosey.

Then Cocky-Locky strutted down into the cave, and he hadn't gone far when "Hrumph!" Cocky-Locky was thrown alongside Turkey-Lurkey, Goosey-Poosey and Ducky-Daddles.

But Cocky-Locky called out to Henny-Penny. And Henny-Penny turned tail and off she ran home; so she never did tell the King the sky was a-falling.

Nicholas Alla

The Three Little Pigs

TRADITIONAL ~ ILLUSTRATED BY ROB LEWIS

Once upon a time there lived an old sow who had three little piglets, and as soon as they were old enough she sent them out into the world to seek their fortunes.

The first little pig met a man carrying a bundle of straw.

"Please, sir, give me that straw to build a house with," said the first little pig. The man gave him the straw and the little pig set to work to build himself a house. It wasn't very strong but it looked good.

No sooner had he finished it than along came a big grey wolf who knocked at the door of the little straw house and said, "Little pig, little pig, let me come in."

"No, no, no, not by the hairs of my chinny chin chin," squeaked the little pig in a great fright.

"Then I'll huff and I'll puff and I'll blow your house in," growled the wolf, and he huffed and he puffed and he blew the house in and gobbled up the little pig.

The second little pig met a man carrying a bundle of sticks.

"Please, sir, give me those sticks to build a house with," said the second little pig. The man gave him the sticks and the little pig soon built himself a little house. It was stronger than the house of straw, but not that strong.

As soon as he was inside, along came the wolf and said, "Little pig, little pig, let me come in."

"No, no, no, not by the hairs of my chinny chin chin," squeaked the little pig, trembling.

"Then I'll huff and I'll puff and I'll blow your house in," growled the wolf, and he huffed and he puffed and he puffed and he huffed and he blew the house in and gobbled up the second little pig.

The third little pig was smarter than the others. He met a man carrying a load of bricks.

"Please, sir, give me those bricks to build a house with," said the third little pig. The man gave him the bricks and soon the little pig had built himself a fine strong house.

The wolf came along to his house too, and knocked on the door, saying, "Little pig, little pig, let me come in."

"No, no, no, not by the hairs of my chinny chin chin," squeaked the little pig, not at all frightened of the wolf.

"Then I'll huff and I'll puff and I'll blow your house in," growled the wolf, and he huffed and he puffed and he puffed and he huffed and he huffed and he puffed, but he could not blow the little brick house in.

So the wolf decided to use trickery. He sat back on his haunches and got his breath back, and then he said, "Little pig, would you like some fine big turnips?"

"Oh yes, I would," said the little pig.

"Then come with me to Farmer Brown's turnip field early tomorrow morning," said the wolf, "and we will collect enough for both of us. I'll come and fetch you at six o'clock."

"Very well," said the little pig, "I'll be ready for you."

But the little pig got up at five o'clock the next morning, and he went to the field, got a great sackful of turnips and was back in his house again before the wolf arrived.

"Little pig, are you ready?" asked the wolf.

"Ready?" answered the little pig. "Why, I've been and come back again and got a nice potful for dinner."

The wolf was very angry, but he made up his mind to catch the little pig somehow, so he said, "Little pig, would you like some nice sweet apples?"

"Yes I would," said the little pig.

"Then come down to the orchard with me tomorrow morning," said the wolf. "And as you get up so early I will call for you at five o'clock."

"I'll be ready," said the little pig.

But he got up at four o'clock and ran down to the orchard, hoping to get back before the wolf arrived. But the wolf had got up early too, and just as the little pig was climbing down the apple tree he saw the wolf coming into the orchard, which did frighten him.

"Are you here before me, little pig?" said the wolf. "And are they nice apples?"

"Yes, very," said the little pig. "I will throw you one down." And he threw it so far that, while the wolf ran down the hill to pick it up, the little pig jumped down from the tree and ran home.

The next day the wolf came again, and said to the little pig, "Little pig, there is a fair in the town this afternoon. Will you come?"

"Oh yes," said the little pig, "I will come. What time will you be ready?"

"At three o'clock," said the wolf.

So the little pig went off before the time, as usual, and got to the fair and bought a butter churn. He was on his way home with it when he saw the wolf coming towards him. So the little pig jumped into the butter churn to hide. The churn toppled over and the pig went rolling down the hill right behind the wolf. This frightened the wolf so much that he ran home without going to the fair.

He went to the little pig's house next day and told him how terrified he had been by a great round thing which came rolling down the hill towards him.

The little pig laughed and said, "Oh, did I frighten you? That was me in my brand new churn."

That made the wolf very angry indeed, and he jumped up on to the roof of the little house, snarling that he would get down the chimney to gobble up the little pig.

When the little pig saw what was happening he made up the fire until it was blazing hot and then he hung a great pot full of water over it. When the wolf came down the chimney the little pig lifted the lid off the pot and the wolf tumbled right into it. Then the little pig clapped the lid back on. And an hour later he gobbled the wolf up, with a scrumptious portion of turnips and apples on the side.

The Emperor's New Clothes

HANS CHRISTIAN ANDERSEN ~
RETOLD AND ILLUSTRATED BY NADINE
BERNARD WESTCOTT

THERE ONCE LIVED an Emperor who was very fond of new clothes. Other kings liked to parade their soldiers or spend an evening at the theatre.

But there was nothing this Emperor loved more than trying on new clothes – which his servants would bring him in great stacks, morning, noon and night.

Other servants toiled endlessly to keep the Emperor's vast wardrobe clean and pressed. The kingdom's most learned scholars were kept constantly on hand to advise him on his choice of clothing. Any outfit the Emperor might desire must be ready for him at a moment's notice.

The Emperor had a different outfit for every hour of the day, and clothes for each day of the week.

For no matter how great or small the occasion, he wanted to wear just the right clothes to make his subjects see him as a wise and able ruler.

But his outfits never seemed quite right.

And his clothes were apt to turn up in the most inconvenient places.

Not even his wife or his most trusted ministers could persuade him that he need not worry so much about his royal attire.

One day, two swindlers travelled to the castle, pretending to be weavers.

"We can weave the most beautiful cloth imaginable!" the first told the Emperor. "And what is more, the clothes from our fabrics are invisible to anyone who is either foolish or unfit for his office."

"Not everyone, of course, is able to wear such finery," added the second. "But they are obviously the perfect clothes for a wise ruler like yourself."

The Emperor thought of how wisely he could rule his people if only he had such an outfit. "Why, not only would I look good but, with those clothes on, I could find out which of my ministers is unfit for his post; I could tell the wise from the foolish. This cloth must be woven for me at once."

The "weavers" set up their looms and worked late into the night.

No one was allowed to see their work until the Emperor sent his wisest and most trusted minister to see what had been made.

The weavers begged the minister to step closer. They named all the colors, and described the pattern in great detail. The minister paid close attention to all they said, for, unable to believe his own eyes, he wanted to be able to repeat it exactly to the Emperor.

The minister hurried back and described the new clothes to the Emperor exactly as they had been described to him.

"Why, you must wear them tomorrow in the royal procession!" the Emperor's wife cried. "It is the perfect chance to show all your subjects what a wise and magnificent ruler you are."

The next morning the weavers at last announced that the clothes were finished. They brought in the royal robes and dressed the Emperor in them, taking great care to see that there were no loose threads and that the royal garments hung just right. The Emperor could scarcely believe his eyes, but he kept quiet as a mouse, lest his subjects should think him a fool.

People had come from every corner of the kingdom to see the magnificent new clothes.

As the Emperor set forth in the royal procession, the crowd grew silent. "My new clothes must be so stunning that no one can find the right words to praise them!" thought the Emperor. He lifted his head and marched on proudly until a small child's voice could be heard clearly to say: "But he has no clothes on!"

"He has no clothes on!" the people echoed, each feeling secretly foolish not to have spoken up earlier.

What could the Emperor possibly do now?

Without any of his royal outfits to help him look intelligent or brave, the Emperor realized it was more important than ever to act like a king.

He lifted his head even higher, and stood even taller, and continued the procession. Never had he felt so foolish ... but never had he acted so wisely.

Seeing their ruler's extraordinary courage, the crowd began to cheer, more loudly than the Emperor had ever heard them.

"Long live the Emperor!"

Red Riding Hood

CHARLES PERRAULT ~ RETOLD AND
ILLUSTRATED BY JAMES MARSHALL

A LONG TIME AGO in a simple cottage beside the deep, dark woods, there lived a pretty child called Red Riding Hood. She was kind and considerate, and everybody loved her.

One afternoon Red Riding Hood's mother called to her. "Granny isn't feeling up to snuff today," she said, "so I've baked her favorite cake as a little surprise. Be a good girl and take it to her, will you?"

Red Riding Hood was delighted. She loved going to Granny's — even though it meant crossing the deep, dark woods.

When the cake had cooled, Red Riding Hood's mother wrapped it up and put it in a basket.

"Now, whatever you do," she said, "go straight to Granny's, do not tarry, do not speak to any strangers."

"Yes, Mama," said Red Riding Hood.

Before long she was in the deepest part of the woods. "Oooh," she said. "This is scary."

Suddenly a large wolf appeared.

"Good afternoon, my dear," he said. "Care to stop for a little chat?"

"Oh, gracious me," said Red Riding Hood. "Mama said not to speak to any strangers."

But the wolf had *such* charming manners. "And where are you going, sweet thing?" he said.

"I'm on my way to visit Granny, who lives in the pretty yellow house on the other side of the woods," said Red Riding Hood. "She's feeling poorly, and I'm taking her a surprise."

"You don't say," said the wolf. Just then he had a delightful idea. "No reason why I can't eat them *both*," he thought. "Allow me to escort you," he said. "You never know what might be lurking about."

"You're too kind," said Red Riding Hood.

Beyond the forest they came to a patch of sunflowers.

"Why not pick a few?" suggested the wolf. "Grannies *love* flowers, you know."

But while Red Riding Hood was picking a pretty bouquet, the clever wolf hurried on ahead to Granny's house.

"Who is it?" called out Granny.

"It is I, your delicious – er – darling granddaughter," said the wolf in a high voice.

"The door is unlocked," said Granny.

"Surprise!" cried the wolf.

Granny was furious at having her reading interrupted. "Get out of here, you horrid thing!" she cried.

But the wolf gobbled her right up. He didn't even bother to chew.

"Tasty," he said, patting his belly, "so tasty." Just then he heard footsteps on the garden path. "Here comes dessert!"

And losing no time, he put on Granny's cap and glasses, jumped into bed, and pulled up the covers.

"Who is it?" he called out in his sweetest granny voice.

"It is I, your little granddaughter," said Red Riding Hood.

"The door is unlocked," said the wolf.

Red Riding Hood was distressed at seeing her grandmother so changed.

"Why, Granny," she said, "what big eyes you have."

"The better to see you, my dear," said the wolf.

"And Granny, what long arms you have."

"The better to hug you, my dear," said the wolf.

"And Granny, what big teeth you have."

"THE BETTER TO EAT YOU, MY DEAR!" cried the wolf. And he gobbled her right up. "I'm so wicked," he said. "*So* wicked." But really he was enormously pleased with himself. And having enjoyed such a heavy meal, he was soon snoring away.

A hunter passing by was alarmed by the frightful racket.

"That doesn't sound like Granny!" he said.

And so the brave hunter jumped in the window, killed the sleeping wolf, and cut him open.

Out jumped Granny and Red Riding Hood.

"We're ever so grateful," said Red Riding Hood.

"That wicked wolf won't trouble you again," said the hunter.

"It was so dark in there I couldn't read a *word*," said Granny.

Red Riding Hood promised never, *ever* to speak to another stranger, charming manners or not.

And she never did.

Jack and the Beanstalk

TRADITIONAL ~ RETOLD AND ILLUSTRATED BY VAL BIRO

ONCE UPON A TIME there was a poor widow who had a son called Jack and a cow called Milky-white. All they had to live on was the milk from the cow. But one day Milky-white gave no more milk and the mother was in despair.

"Cheer up, Mother," said Jack. "We can sell the cow and then we'll see what we can do." So he took the halter and led Milky-white off to market.

On the way he met a gnarled old man with twinkly eyes.

"Well now," said the old man, "you look like a smart lad. I wonder if you know how many beans make five?"

"Two in each hand and one in your mouth," said Jack, as sharp as a needle.

"In that case," twinkled the old man, "here are the very beans themselves. They are magic, mind, and if you plant them overnight they'll reach the sky by morning. I'll swap them for your cow."

"Magic beans for an old cow! Now *that* was a good bargain," thought Jack, handing over Milky-white and pocketing the beans. He was sharp right enough.

"Beans?" shrieked his mother when he got home. "Five dried-up miserable beans for a cow? You are an idiot! Nincompoop! Dunderhead! Take that! And that! As for your precious beans, here they go out of the window!" She was beside herself with rage and sent Jack to bed without any supper.

So Jack shuffled upstairs, hungry and miserable.

But when he woke next morning he stared in amazement. His room was bathed in green light, shaded by great big leaves right outside his window. The leaves of a huge beanstalk that reached the sky! So the old man had been right after all.

Jack opened the window, jumped on to the beanstalk, and began to climb.

He climbed and he climbed and he climbed, until at last he reached the sky. And when he got there he found himself on a rocky road leading to a great big castle.

A great big woman stood there. Jack was hungry after his climb, so he asked her politely for some breakfast.

"Breakfast?" she boomed. "It's breakfast you'll be if you don't move off. My husband's an ogre and he likes to eat boys on toast!"

But she took pity on him, and led him into the kitchen. Jack wasn't halfway through his meal when thump! thump! thump! the castle began to shake.

"My old man's coming!" wailed the old woman and bundled Jack into the oven.

In came the huge ogre, sniffing.

"*Fee-fi-fo-fum,*
I smell the blood of an Englishman,
Be he alive or be he dead,
I'll grind his bones to make my bread."

"Nonsense, dear," said his wife, "you're dreaming. Just sit down and have your breakfast. You'll feel better then."

Well, the ogre had his breakfast, and after that he went to a chest, took out two bags of gold, sat down again and began to count. Soon he fell asleep, snoring enough to shake the rafters.

Then Jack crept out on tiptoe from his oven, put one of the bags of gold over his shoulder, and off he pelted. He climbed down the beanstalk, down and down, until at last he got home.

"Well, Mother, wasn't I right about the beans? They *were* magical, you see!"

So they lived on the gold for some time, but at last it ran out and Jack decided to try his luck again.

Up the beanstalk he climbed, up and up, until he saw the great big woman again.

"Aren't you the boy who came here once before?" she asked. "That very day my ogre missed one of his bags of gold."

"That's strange," said Jack. "I dare say I could tell you something about that, but I can't speak till I've had something to eat."

Well, the great big woman was so curious that she took him indoors and gave him breakfast.

Jack had hardly finished when thump! thump! thump! the castle began to shake again. "Quick!" said the woman and hid Jack in the cupboard.

"*Fee-fi-fo-fum*," said the huge ogre sniffing around, looking very suspicious. But then he sat down to have his breakfast. After that he asked his wife to bring in the speckled hen, and she put it on the table.

"*Lay!*" said the ogre, and the hen laid an egg all of gold.

The ogre pocketed it, yawned and began to snore till the whole castle shook.

Jack crept out on tiptoe from his cupboard, took the speckled hen under his arm and ran away. But the hen gave a cackle and woke the ogre who began to shout. That was all Jack heard, because he was off and down that beanstalk like a shot.

Well, Jack and his mother became rich, what with a golden egg every time they said "Lay!" But Jack was not content, and before long he determined to try his luck for a third time.

So one fine morning he climbed up the beanstalk, and he climbed and he climbed.

And when he reached the great big castle he hid behind a bush until he saw the ogre's wife come out with a pail. Then Jack tiptoed into the castle and hid under the lid of a cauldron.

Thump! thump! thump! he heard and in came the ogre and his wife. "*Fee-fi-fo-fum, I smell the blood of an Englishman,*" roared the ogre and sniffed around the oven, the cupboard and everything, only luckily he didn't think of the cauldron. So he sat down to breakfast.

Then his wife brought in a golden harp and the ogre said, "*Sing!*" And the harp sang most beautifully till the ogre fell asleep.

Jack crept out on tiptoe from his cauldron, caught hold of the golden harp and dashed off towards the door. But the harp called out: "Master! Master!" and the ogre woke up just in time to see Jack running off.

Jack ran as fast as he could, but the
ogre came thundering after. He would soon have
caught up, only Jack reached the beanstalk first and started climbing
down for dear life. Just then the harp cried out: "Master! Master!" and
when the ogre heard this he swung himself down the beanstalk too.

By this time Jack had climbed down and climbed down and climbed down till he was very nearly home. But the ogre came down after him, came down and came down, and the beanstalk was wobbling under his weight like a jelly. So Jack called out: "Mother! Mother! Bring me an axe!" And his mother came rushing out with the axe and stared in horror to see the ogre's legs sticking through the clouds.

Jack jumped down and chopped at the beanstalk with the axe. He chopped and he chopped until the beanstalk was cut in two. With a terrible cry the ogre came tumbling down and broke his crown. There was a great big hole where he fell and the beanstalk came toppling after him. And that was that.

So what with the golden harp that sang, the speckled hen that laid golden eggs, and all that money, Jack and his mother lived happily ever after.

The Elves and the Shoemaker

The Brothers Grimm ~ Retold and
Illustrated by Bernadette Watts

ONCE UPON A TIME, through sheer bad luck, an honest shoemaker became so poor that he had nothing left in his workshop except enough leather to make a single pair of shoes. Although he was very tired, the good man cut out the shoes and laid the pieces on the workbench ready to sew them the next day. Then he went to bed and slept peacefully.

The next morning the shoemaker went into his workshop and there, to his great surprise, he saw a finished pair of shoes!

He looked at the shoes carefully. He examined the soles and the uppers, but he could not find one careless stitch. They were perfect!

Early that day a customer came along. The shoes delighted him and were exactly what he needed. In fact, he was so pleased he paid a very good price.

With this money the shoemaker bought fresh food for himself and his family, and enough fine leather to make two more pairs of shoes.

That evening, with renewed energy, the shoemaker cut out the leather shapes for two pairs of shoes. Then, feeling content, he went to bed.

The shoemaker rose early the next morning to start work, but there was no need! For there on the workbench were two pairs of shoes, as beautifully sewn as the first.

Customers soon came along and paid good prices for the shoes. Then the shoemaker bought enough leather for four more pairs.

Overnight the four pairs were made. And so it went on. Whatever he cut out in the evening was finished the next morning. Soon he was a wealthy man again.

After finishing work one evening, just before Christmas, the shoemaker said to his wife: "Shall we stay up tonight, to find out who has been helping us?"

His wife liked the idea. So they lit a candle, hid behind some clothes which were hanging on pegs, and kept watch.

At midnight, two little elves came in. They jumped on to the workbench, gathered up the cut-out leather and then began to stitch and sew and hammer with

such skill and speed the shoemaker was amazed. The elves worked hard without stopping. When the shoes were completely finished they hurried away.

The next morning the shoemaker's wife said: "The elves have made us rich, and we really must show our gratitude. They must be so cold, running about without a stitch of clothes to wear. I have an idea! I will make them each a shirt, a jacket, a vest, a pair of trousers, and I'll knit them each a pair of warm stockings. And you can make them each a pair of fine shoes."

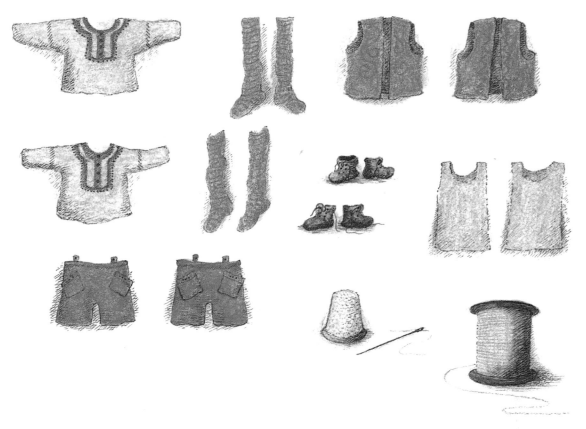

"That's an excellent plan!" agreed the shoemaker. So, on Christmas Eve, instead of laying out the leather they arranged their gifts on the table. Then they hid and waited for the elves to arrive.

At midnight the elves came bounding in, eager to get to work. But they found no leather, only the pretty little clothes and shoes. At first they were puzzled. Then they were delighted! They dressed quickly and then they jumped around and sang:

"Now we are boys so fine to see,
Why should we longer cobblers be!"

They danced and skipped around the room. Finally they danced out of the door and disappeared.

The elves never returned. But as long as the shoemaker lived, everything went well for him and all his efforts were rewarded.

Cinderella

CHARLES PERRAULT ~ RETOLD BY KATHLEEN LINES
AND ILLUSTRATED BY SHIRLEY HUGHES

ONCE UPON A TIME there lived a gentleman who married, as his second wife, a handsome widow. She was however an excessively proud and ill-natured woman, and her two daughters were just like her. The man, on his side, also had a daughter, younger than her step-sisters, and she, taking after her own mother, was gentle, sweet and charming.

The wedding festivities were barely over when the woman showed her true character. She began to ill-treat her step-daughter, whose beauty and goodness made her own daughters seem all the more unattractive. The poor child was given all the rough household tasks to do. And while her step-sisters were surrounded with every comfort and luxury and lived a life of ease, the younger girl swept and dusted their rooms, washed the dishes, scrubbed the floor and steps and worked from morning till night. Her room was a wretched attic at the top of the house, and her bed a mattress filled with straw. She bore all this hardship with patience, not daring to complain to her father lest he should scold her, for he was quite under the thumb of his new wife.

In the evening when her work was finished the poor girl would sit in the chimney corner among the ashes and embers for warmth, and because of this she was called Cinderella. However, in spite of her hard life and the ragged clothes she was forced to wear, Cinderella was still a hundred times more beautiful than her step-sisters, although they were always magnificently dressed.

Now it happened that the King's son was giving two balls, to which all persons of fashion were invited. Of course the two young ladies received an invitation, for they went out much into society. They were delighted, and for weeks did nothing but talk about what they would wear. Cinderella was kept very busy washing and ironing and sewing for them. They ordered elaborate head-dresses from their best milliner, and the most expensive beauty preparations.

Cinderella was called upon to help and advise them, for she had excellent taste. She arranged their hair most expertly even though they cruelly teased her, asking if she would not like to go to the balls, and saying how everyone would laugh to see a Cinder-wench among the fine ladies.

At last the happy moment for departure came, and off they went. Cinderella followed them with her eyes for as long as she could, and when they were out of sight she sat down by the fireside and burst into tears. At that moment her fairy godmother appeared beside her. "What

is the matter, dear child?" she said. "Why do you cry so bitterly?"

"I wish – oh, I wish …" Cinderella began, but tears choked her and she could not go on.

"You wish that you could go to the ball, is that it?" asked her godmother.

"Oh, yes I do," sobbed Cinderella.

"Well," said the old lady, "you are a good girl and I shall see to it. Go into the garden and fetch me a pumpkin."

Cinderella did as she was bid and brought the largest pumpkin she could find, but wondering all the while what use it could be. Her godmother scooped out the inside, leaving nothing but the rind, and then touched it with her wand. Instantly it became a splendid golden coach. After that she looked in the mousetrap, and found there six live mice. She told Cinderella to lift up the trap door gently, and as the mice ran out one by one she tapped each one with her wand and it was turned into a horse. So here was a team of six dapple-grey carriage horses, only needing a coachman. "I'll go and look at the rat-trap," said Cinderella. "If there is a rat in it, we'll make a coachman of him."

"You are right," said her godmother, "go and see." There were three rats in the trap. The old lady chose the one with the longest whiskers, and at the touch of her wand it became a fat jolly coachman with a splendid moustache. Then she told Cinderella to fetch the six lizards she would find behind the water-butt. These were changed into six footmen, wearing smart livery, who at once climbed up behind the coach as though they had done nothing else all their lives.

"There now," said her godmother, "you have your coach and all that is necessary to go to the ball. Are you pleased?"

"Oh, yes, dear godmother," answered Cinderella. "But must I go dressed as I am in these ugly, ragged clothes?"

Her godmother only just touched Cinderella with her wand, and in an instant her rags became a beautiful ball-gown made of cloth of gold and silver, and all sparkling with jewels. The old lady then gave her a pair of exquisite little glass slippers to put on. And now Cinderella got up into the coach ready to set out for the palace. But before she left her godmother solemnly warned her to be home before the clock struck twelve. At one minute after midnight her coach would become a pumpkin again, the horses mice, the footmen lizards and Cinderella would find herself in her old clothes once more. Cinderella promised to

obey her godmother, and joyfully
drove off to the ball.

The prince, who had been told that an
unknown princess had arrived, himself hurried out to receive her. He
gave her his hand as she alighted from the coach and led her into the
great hall where all the guests were dancing. When Cinderella entered the

ballroom there was a moment's complete silence. Talking ceased, the dancers stood still, and the violinists stopped playing – then there was a growing murmur, "Oh, how beautiful she is, how beautiful she is." Even the old King gazed on her with delight and said softly to the Queen that it was many years since he had seen such a lovely young creature. All the women carefully studied her appearance in every detail, with the intention of dressing in the same way themselves, if such materials and clever dressmakers could be found.

The prince led Cinderella to a place of honor, and later he danced with her. A splendid supper was served but the prince was so lost in admiration of her grace and beauty that he could eat nothing. Cinderella went and sat with her sisters and was most gracious and pleasant, even sharing with them fruit that the prince had given her. This kindness astonished them for they did not recognize her. Then Cinderella heard the clock strike eleven and three-quarters so she got up, made a curtsey to the company and quickly left the palace.

She found her godmother waiting for her at home. After thanking her for a happy evening she pleaded to be allowed to go again to the ball next

day, since the prince had particularly asked her. While she was telling her godmother everything that had occurred, her sisters returned. The fairy vanished and Cinderella went to open the door. "You are very late," she said, yawning and rubbing her eyes, as if she had just that moment woken up; although in truth she had not for one moment during their absence thought of sleep.

"If you had been to the ball," said one of the sisters, "you would not have wished to leave any earlier. The most beautiful princess in the world was there."

"Yes," said the other, "and she sat by us and was very attentive."

Cinderella feigned indifference, but asked the name of the princess.

"No one knows," they answered, "and the King's son would give the world to find out who she is."

At this Cinderella sighed, and said, "How I wish I could see the beautiful princess."

The next evening the two sisters went again to the ball. Cinderella was there too, and was dressed even more splendidly than before. The prince was constantly by her side, paying her compliments and speaking tender words to her. He danced with no one else  all evening. Cinderella was so happy that the time passed all too quickly, and she forgot her godmother's warning. The clock began to strike. "It could only be eleven," she thought. But it was twelve o'clock! Cinderella jumped up and ran, swiftly as a deer. The prince followed her but did not catch her. In her flight Cinderella dropped one of her little glass slippers, and this the prince picked up carefully and carried, while he hunted everywhere for her in vain. The guards were questioned, but none had seen the princess leave.

Cinderella arrived home quite out of breath, without coach or footmen, and in her old clothes. Nothing was left of her finery but a little glass slipper, fellow to the one she had dropped.

When her step-sisters returned, Cinderella asked if the strange princess had been at the ball.

"Yes," they answered, "but she left as soon as the clock struck midnight, and in such haste that she dropped one of her little glass slippers. The prince has it." Then they told her that the prince must be very much in love with the owner of the slipper since he had looked at no one else the whole evening.

They spoke truly, for a few days later it was proclaimed to the sound of trumpets that the prince would marry the

one whose foot the glass slipper exactly fitted. What excitement there was! The Court Chamberlain visited princesses first, and then the duchesses and after that the ladies of the court, but all to no purpose. At last he came to Cinderella's step-sisters. Each one tried and tried to force her foot into the little slipper, but in vain. It was far too small.

Cinderella, who was watching and knew her own slipper, said

lightly, "Let me see if it will fit." The two sisters burst out laughing and began to jeer at her. But the Chamberlain, looking at her closely, saw that she was very pretty and he said he had orders that all girls should try on the slipper and it was only right that she should have her chance. So he made Cinderella sit down and hold out her foot, and the little slipper went on easily and fitted as perfectly as if it had been moulded to her foot in wax.

The step-sisters were astonished, but they were even more astounded when Cinderella took the other slipper from her pocket and put it on. At that moment her fairy godmother appeared, and with a touch of her wand changed Cinderella's rags into more magnificent clothes than any she had worn before.

Then the step-sisters knew that Cinderella was the beautiful princess they had seen at the ball. They fell on their knees before her to beg forgiveness for their harsh and unkind treatment. She raised them up,

and, as she kissed them, said that she forgave them with all her heart, and hoped they would always love her.

Cinderella was conducted to the prince. Their wedding took place the very next day.

Then Cinderella, who was as good as she was beautiful, brought her sisters to the palace, and soon married them to two noblemen of the court.

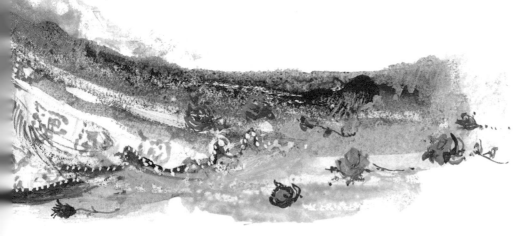

When Dreams Came True

The Selfish Giant

OSCAR WILDE ~ RETOLD AND ILLUSTRATED
BY ALLISON REED

T HERE WAS ONCE a giant who came down from the mountains to build himself a castle in the valley. All the people of the valley were amazed by the beauty of his castle and the garden that surrounded it. Flowers of every scent and color grew there, and birds and butterflies flew everywhere. It seemed there was magic in the garden and in the afternoons after school the children would go there to play.

One day the giant dug up a tree as a present and set off up the steep mountain path to visit his friend. His friend was delighted to see him and the two giants sat talking for days and days. The giant told his friend all about his wonderful garden. "But surely," his friend said, "it cannot be the most beautiful garden in the world if you let all the children trample on it." And the giant saw some sense in what his friend said.

The next day the giants climbed to the very top of the mountain and found the biggest boulder anyone had ever seen.

"This will build a fine wall," his friend said.

And the giant set off home struggling under the weight of the enormous boulder.

After many days the giant reached the valley. With his left hand he smashed the great stone and laid the pieces one upon the other to build a great wall around the garden. It was autumn by the time the wall was finished. The giant stood back to admire his work and thought, "Now it really is my garden. No one will be able to spoil it."

Outside the garden, the children had nowhere to play. They wandered round the high walls when their lessons were over and talked about the beautiful garden inside.

"How happy we were there," they said to each other.

Winter came, and the garden was bleak and white and silent. The giant stared at the snow and longed for spring.

Months went by and there was no sign of a thaw. Little did the giant know that outside his wall the sun shone and the grass was green. Then one morning, the giant was woken by the song of a bird.

"At last," he cried, "spring is here."

He looked out of the window and saw that the snow was melting. In a corner of the garden the children had made a hole in his great wall. Laughing and shouting they ran happily into the garden. Everything came to life again. Flowers bloomed and the grass was green.

The giant hurried down to greet the children but when they saw him coming they ran away to hide. Only the smallest boy remained. He stood crying under a tree whose branches still had no leaves. The giant gently lifted him up and as the boy's small hands touched the branches the tree burst into blossom. "How selfish I have been," thought the giant. "With my great wall I have locked the spring out of my garden."

The children who had been watching came out from their hiding places. They shyly gathered round the giant and offered him flowers.

"It is your garden now, children," said the giant. And together they started to break down the great wall. With the stones they built arches and the children ran round and round and in and out of them.

The giant saw that his garden was more beautiful than ever. He loved all the children but he kept a special place in his heart for the smallest child. For it was he who had shown the giant how his selfishness had destroyed his garden. From that day until the end of the giant's life the children played happily in the garden.

Puss in Boots

CHARLES PERRAULT ~ RETOLD AND
ILLUSTRATED BY TONY ROSS

Long, long ago, a miller lived in a mill with his three sons. The eldest son was called Lazy Harry, the second eldest was called Good-for-Nothing Tom, and the youngest was called Jack. The miller also had a cat with wild yellow eyes. His name was Puss.

Young Jack did all the work, but he did it happily, and loved everyone and everything. He was sad when the old miller fell sick.

When the miller died he left the mill to Harry, the horse to Tom, and the cat to Jack. Jack felt that perhaps he was not so lucky.

"Never mind," whispered Puss. "I may be able to make your fortune, but first you must buy me some boots." So Jack took him to the boot shop.

Puss tried on all sorts of boots and shoes, and in the end he chose a pair of high boots, made from yellow leather. They made him look much taller.

"Now," he said to Jack, "you must buy me a bag that I can carry on my back."

So Jack took the cat to the scout shop and bought one of their finest rucksacks. It had leather straps, and was waterproof.

That night, Puss went to a lettuce field and filled his bag with lettuce. He went into the woods and laid the lettuce on the ground. Then he hid.

In no time at all, a fat rabbit appeared out of his hole and saw the line of lettuce. Being greedy as well as fat, the rabbit gobbled them up, not knowing how close it was getting to the cat.

Just as the rabbit was stretching out a paw for the last lettuce, Puss leaped out and caught it in the bag.

Chuckling to himself, Puss set off along a winding path, carefully following the signposts.

Soon the cat arrived at the King's castle and walked boldly up to the guard at the gate.

"No catsdogspigssheepormonsters allowed!" snapped the guard.

"May not a cat look at a king?" whispered Puss, and seeing no harm in it, the guard marched him towards the throne room. The King blinked to see a cat in yellow boots.

"Your Majesty," said Puss, bowing low, "please accept this fine rabbit, a gift from the estate of my master, the Marquis of Carabas."

The King was most impressed, with both the rabbit and the polite cat. "Do thank your master," he said, and the cat left the castle, a friend of the King.

Puss trotted away, pleased with his work.

The next day, Puss took some corn and laid it in a trail. Then he lay down and pretended to be dead. When two partridges came along, eating the corn, he popped them in his bag too.

Again he visited the King, saying that the partridges were gifts from his master. The King was well pleased. On his way out, Puss met the secretary and found out where the King's coach was to pass the next day.

Next morning, Puss told Jack that he was to swim in the river.

"Don't want to," sniffed Jack. "It'll be *freezing!*"

"Trust me, and remember that I'll make your fortune," wheedled the crafty cat. Jack, being a simple lad, agreed, and dived into the river.

It *was* freezing. "Funny way to make a fortune!" he gasped to Puss, who sat warm and dry on the bank.

Puss knew that the King's coach was going to pass that way, so when Jack wasn't looking, he hid his clothes, then ran into the road and stopped the royal coach.

"HELP! HELP!" he howled. "My master, the Marquis of Carabas, is drowning!"

The King jumped out of his coach, followed by his daughter. Waving

his arms, he told the coachman to go and help the marquis.

"But he has no clothes!" said the cat. "His silks were stolen by a band of wicked thieves."

Of course, Jack's clothes were not really silk; they were the old rags he had worn for years.

When the coachman returned with Jack, the lad was so cold he couldn't speak. A chest of royal clothes was produced, and Jack was given a suit of the finest cloth. He looked every inch a marquis. When the King thanked him for the rabbit and the partridges, Jack hadn't the faintest idea what he was talking about, but he was too cold to argue. (Puss had found a very nice hat for himself.)

The King allowed Jack to ride in the royal

coach, which pleased the princess, who was falling in love with the Marquis of Carabas.

As the coach went on its way, the cat ran ahead, and soon he came to a cornfield where harvesters were cutting the corn.

"Listen!" shouted Puss, in his sternest voice. "When the royal coach comes by, you must say that all these fields belong to the Marquis of

Carabas. If you don't, I'll come back and scratch you to bits. OK?"

"OK!" said the harvesters, badly frightened.

Puss then went on until he came across a goatherd.

"When the King comes by, you must tell him that these goats belong to the Marquis of Carabas. If you don't, I'll come back and pull your beard. OK?"

"OK!" gasped the surprised goatherd.

Puss rushed on his way, towards a white palace in the forest.

Puss strode right up to the front door of the palace and banged loudly on the knocker. It was quite a brave thing to do, as a terrible ogre lived there. The ogre opened the door himself. (He had to, as he had eaten all his servants.)

The ogre didn't have many visitors on account of his bad temper, and he blinked at the cat in yellow boots peeping in through his door.

"Greetings, Your Ugliness," smiled Puss. "I have long wanted to meet you. I have heard you can turn yourself into any animal you please. The thing is, I just don't believe it!"

The ogre couldn't believe his ears. He spluttered and coughed, and jumped up and down in a rage.

"Gggglumph, I can, I can too! Glummmph, I'll show you, I'll show you, then I'll chew you!"

His hair grew, and slowly the ogre changed into a terrible lion.

With a leap, the lion chased Puss up the chimney.

"Pooh! I don't think *that's* so smart," yelled Puss from the safety of the chimney. "Everyone can grow big, that's *easy*! Can't you do better? Can't you turn into something small?"

The lion seemed quite put out, so Puss dropped down out of the chimney.

"Like a mouse," the sneaky cat said with a grin. "Could you change into a mouse?"

"Er, yes, I think so," muttered the ogre. "Changing into lions is quite difficult, you know!"

The ogre grew smaller and smaller, and mousier and mousier.

When his roars turned into squeaks and he was really quite tiny, Puss pounced!

And swallowed the terrible ogre in one mousey gulp!

In the meantime, the King arrived at the cornfields.

"To whom do these fields belong?" said the King to the harvesters.

"To the Marquis of Carabas," they answered.

Then the royal coach passed the goatherd, and the King asked who owned the fine goats.

"The Marquis of Carabas, Sire," said the goatherd, shaking.

"You really are a most important marquis!" said the King to Jack, who still hadn't the faintest idea what he was talking about.

When the King arrived at the white palace, he was lost in admiration.

"Who owns this wonderful palace?" he said to Puss, who met them at the gate.

"The Marquis of Carabas, my master," said the cat.

Puss had prepared a banquet for the King, who, having eaten, turned to Jack and said: "My dear Marquis of Carabas, all of this splendor is too much for a marquis, I will make you a prince."

Although Jack still didn't quite understand what was going on, he dropped on one knee, and the King tapped him on the shoulder.

"Arise, Jack, Prince of Carabas."

Of course, Jack married the King's daughter, and they lived long lives in the white palace. He loved the princess and enjoyed being a real prince.

In gratitude, he made Puss the Master of the Prince's Household, and Grand Mouser in Chief ... although he *still* didn't understand some of the things Puss did.

The Sorcerer's Apprentice

JOHANN WOLFGANG VON GOETHE ~ RETOLD BY LAURA CECIL
AND ILLUSTRATED BY EMMA CHICHESTER CLARK

A SORCERER LIVED IN A LONELY HOUSE on the side of a mountain. He was a formidable old man with a bowed back and thick red spectacles that hid his eyes. Now that he was old, he needed an apprentice to help him, so he found a boy who was sharp-witted and eager to learn. At first the boy, whose name was Felix, enjoyed his work. He was fascinated by the strange herbs he had to collect and by the ancient glass jars filled with bubbling mixtures in his master's room. But soon he longed to be able to work spells himself. Yet whenever he asked the sorcerer to teach him, he was told that he was too young and that magic was dangerous. He must be patient and wait until he had learned more. Felix did not answer back, but he thought to himself: "The old fool doesn't want me to learn in case I get the better of him. I'll watch him carefully and learn that way."

So, day after day, he watched and listened. At night he would creep down and study the sorcerer's books when the old man was asleep. He was especially interested by the way the sorcerer was able to summon up spirits to make the things in his work-room come alive and help him with

his magic. At his command the glass jars full of bubbling mixtures would rise up and pour themselves into other vessels, and stop as soon as he spoke another magic word. The sorcerer's favorite object was an old broomstick that he used to help him carry out tasks he thought too difficult or dangerous for Felix. He spoke his magic commands very fast and it was some time before Felix could understand them and learn the words by heart. He longed to try out what he knew, but he did not dare while the sorcerer was in the house.

Then one day the sorcerer announced that he had to go out on urgent business. "We have a very important spell to make tonight. I want you to prepare it while I am out. You must fill the marble tub in the middle of my work-room with fresh water from the stream outside. Make sure it is full by the time I return." So saying he clambered on to a small dragon and flew away.

"At last he's gone!" said Felix. "Now I shall be able to call up spirits too! It will take me all day to fill that tub if I carry the water from the stream myself, so let's see what I can use to help me!"

He looked round the work-room and saw his master's broomstick leaning against the wall. He pointed at it and said the magic words of command:

> *"Quick, quick, Magic Broomstick,*
> *To the stream you must run,*
> *Bring water in bucketfuls one by one*
> *Till the tub be filled as I have willed."*

The broomstick quivered. Its twigs divided into two feet, thin arms sprang out of the handle and a small head grew out of the top. Felix thrust a bucket into its hand and it strode out of the door making a curious rustling sound with its twiggy feet. A moment later it was back from the stream and filling the tub. Back and forth it went, quicker and quicker. "This is better than I could have hoped," thought Felix. "The job will soon be done and I will have lots of time to try out other spells."

He began to study his master's books, but suddenly a slopping noise made him look up. The tub was almost full, but the broom still rustled back and forth emptying the bucket until the tub began to overflow. "Still stand – I mean – stand still, O Broom!" cried Felix.

Then he realized to his horror that he could not remember the rest of the spell. Frantically, he searched his master's books for the words. Meanwhile the broom worked quicker and quicker. The tub flooded over on to the floor and soon Felix was ankle-deep in water. But still the broom worked on. It was able to glide on top of the water so that now it made a swishing sound instead of a rustling one.

Felix tried every spell he could remember, but not one had the right words. "Oh, how I wish you were an old broomstick again!" he moaned. "There's nothing for it, I'll have to catch you and force you to stop or I shall be drowned."

As the broom swooshed past, Felix grabbed it. The broom turned its head and bit him sharply so that he let go immediately, crying with pain. Its hard wooden eyes glared at him malevolently, but it never slackened its pace. Felix was terrified. What would the sorcerer say when he came back? Already the water had spread to other rooms, and books and bottles were floating round him higgledy-piggledy.

Then Felix saw an axe hanging on the wall behind him. He seized it and when the broom came by again he aimed a careful blow and split it deftly down the middle. Sighing with relief, Felix flopped down in a puddle of soggy papers. At last the broom had been stopped. Then to his horror he saw the two halves of the broom stand up. Each one now had two twiggy feet, two arms and a malevolent little head on top of the handle. They each seized a bucket and set off for the stream. Now there was twice as much water coming into the house.

Felix tried to snatch the buckets as the brooms strode past but they were too fast for him. Then he seized another bucket and tried to carry some of the water out again, but all to no avail. The brooms only worked faster when they saw what he was trying to do.

Then suddenly he remembered a summoning spell. Desperately, Felix called upon the sorcerer to appear. There was a clatter of wings and a hiss of steam as the dragon and sorcerer landed in the water before him. The sorcerer raised his arms and seemed to grow twice as tall.

"Stand still, O Broom and Broom!
Return to your corner of the room!
Never again shall you live
Until you hear ME orders give!
Flood, begone!
Go back to the stream where you belong."

Instantly the water vanished, the brooms dropped the buckets and hopped into the corner. A second later they fused into one broomstick again which fell with a lifeless clatter against the wall. The sorcerer picked it up and handed it to Felix. "Now you can use this to sweep up all the mess," he said. "But no more magic."

The Ugly Duckling

HANS CHRISTIAN ANDERSEN ~ TRANSLATED BY
ERIK HAUGAARD AND ILLUSTRATED BY
ALISON CATLEY

IT WAS SO beautiful out in the country. It was summer. The oats were still green, but the wheat was turning yellow. Down in the meadow the grass had been cut and made into haystacks; and there the storks walked on their long red legs talking Egyptian, because that was the language they had been taught by their mothers. The fields were enclosed by woods, and hidden among them were little lakes and pools. Yes, it certainly was lovely out there in the country!

The old castle, with its deep moat surrounding it, lay bathed in sunshine. Between the heavy walls and the edge of the moat there was a narrow strip of land covered by a whole forest of burdock plants. Their leaves were large and some of the stalks were so tall that a child could stand upright under them and imagine that he was in the middle of the wild and lonely woods. Here a duck had built her nest. While she sat waiting for the eggs to hatch, she felt a little sorry for herself because it was taking so long and hardly anybody came to visit her. The other ducks preferred swimming in the moat to sitting under a dock leaf and gossiping.

Finally the eggs began to crack. "Peep ... Peep," they said one after another. The egg yolks had become alive and were sticking out their heads.

"Quack ... Quack ..." said their mother. "Look around you." And the ducklings did; they glanced at the green world about them, and that was what their mother wanted them to do, for green was good for their eyes.

"How big the world is!" piped the little ones, for they had much more space to move around in now than they had had inside the egg.

"Do you think that this is the whole world?" quacked their mother. "The world is much larger than this. It stretches as far as the minister's wheat fields, though I have not been there ... Are you all here?" The duck got up and turned round to look at her nest. "Oh no, the biggest egg hasn't hatched yet; and I'm so tired of sitting here! I wonder how long it will take?" she wailed, and sat down again.

"What's new?" asked an old duck who had come visiting.

"One of the eggs is taking so long," complained the mother duck. "It won't crack. But take a look at the others. They are the sweetest little ducklings you have ever seen; and every one of them looks exactly like their father. That scoundrel hasn't come to visit me once."

"Let me look at the egg that won't hatch," demanded the old duck. "I am sure that it's a turkey egg! I was fooled that way once. You can't imagine what it's like. Turkeys are afraid of the water. I couldn't get them to go into it. I quacked and I nipped them, but nothing helped. Let me see that egg! ... Yes, it's a turkey egg. Just let it lie there. You go and teach your young ones how to swim, that's my advice."

"I have sat on it so long that I suppose I can sit a little longer, at least until they get the hay in," replied the mother duck.

"Suit yourself," said the older duck, and went on.

At last the big egg cracked too. "Peep ... Peep," said the young one, and tumbled out. He was big and very ugly.

The mother duck looked at him. "He's awfully big for his age," she said. "He doesn't look like any of the others. I wonder if he could be a turkey? Well, we shall soon see. Into the water he will go, even if I have to kick him to make him do it."

The next day the weather was gloriously beautiful. The sun shone on the forest of burdock plants. The mother duck took her whole brood to the moat. "Quack ... Quack ..." she ordered.

One after another, the little ducklings plunged into the water. For a moment their heads disappeared, but then they popped up again and the little ones floated like so many corks. Their legs knew what to do without being told. All of the new brood swam very nicely, even the ugly one.

"He is no turkey," mumbled the mother. "See how beautifully he uses his legs and how straight he holds his neck. He is my own child and, when you look closely at him, he's quite handsome ... Quack! Quack! Follow me and I'll take you to the henyard and introduce you to everyone. But stay close to me, so that no one steps on you, and look out for the cat."

They heard an awful noise when they arrived at the henyard. Two families of ducks had got into a fight over the head of an eel. Neither of them got it, for it was swiped by the cat.

"That is the way of the world," said the mother duck, and licked her bill. She would have liked to have had the eel's head herself. "Walk nicely," she admonished them. "And remember to bow to the old duck over there. She has Spanish blood in her veins and is the most aristocratic fowl here. That is why she is so fat and has a red rag tied round one of her legs. That is the highest mark of distinction a duck can be given. It means so much that she will never be done away with; and all the other fowl and the human beings know who she is. Quack! Quack! ... Don't walk, waddle like well brought up ducklings. Keep your legs far apart, just as your mother and father have always done. Bow your heads and say, 'Quack!'" And that was what the little ducklings did.

Other ducks gathered about them and said loudly, "What do we want that gang here for? Aren't there enough of us already? Pooh! Look how ugly one of them is! He's the last straw!" And one of the ducks flew over and bit the ugly duckling on the neck.

"Leave him alone!" shouted the mother. "He hasn't done anyone any harm."

"He's big and he doesn't look like everybody else!" replied the duck who had bitten him. "And that's reason enough to beat him."

"Very good-looking children you have," remarked the duck with the red rag round one of her legs. "All of them are beautiful except one. He didn't turn out very well. I wish you could make him over again."

"That's not possible, Your Grace," answered the mother duck. "He may not be handsome, but he has a good character and swims as well as the others, if not a little better. Perhaps he will grow handsomer as he grows older and becomes a bit smaller. He was in the egg too long, and that is why he doesn't have the right shape." She smoothed his neck for a moment and then added, "Besides, he's a drake; and it doesn't matter so much what he looks like. He is strong and I am sure he will be able to take care of himself."

"Well, the others are nice," said the old duck. "Make yourself at home, and if you should find an eel's head, you may bring it to me."

And they were "at home".

The poor little duckling, who had been the last to hatch and was so ugly, was bitten and pushed and made fun of both by the hens and by the other ducks. The turkey cock (who had been born with spurs on, and therefore thought he was an emperor) rustled his feathers as if he were a full-rigged ship under sail, and strutted up to the duckling. He gobbled so loudly at him that his own face got all red.

The poor little duckling did not know where to turn. How he grieved

over his own ugliness, and how sad he was! The poor creature was mocked and laughed at by the whole henyard.

That was the first day; and each day that followed was worse than the one before. The poor duckling was chased and mistreated by everyone, even his own sisters and brothers, who quacked again and again, "If only the cat would get you, you ugly thing!"

Even his mother said, "I wish you were far away." The other ducks bit him and the hens pecked at him. The little girl who came to feed the fowls kicked him.

At last the duckling ran away. He flew over the tops of the bushes, frightening all the little birds so that they flew up into the air. "They, too, think I am ugly," thought the duckling, and closed his eyes — but he kept on running.

Finally he came to a great swamp where wild ducks lived; and here he stayed for the night, for he was too tired to go any farther.

In the morning he was discovered by the wild ducks. They looked at him and one of them asked, "What kind of bird are you?"

The ugly duckling bowed in all directions, for he was trying to be as polite as he knew how.

"You are ugly," said the wild ducks, "but that is no concern of ours, as long as you don't try to marry into our family."

The poor duckling wasn't thinking of marriage. All he wanted was to be allowed to swim among the reeds and drink a little water when he was thirsty.

He spent two days in the swamp; then two wild geese came — or rather, two wild ganders, for they were males. They had been hatched not long ago; therefore they were both frank and bold.

"Listen, comrade," they said. "You are so ugly that we like you. Do you want to migrate with us? Not far from here there is a marsh where some beautiful wild geese live. They are all lovely maidens, and you are so ugly that you may seek your fortune among them. Come along."

"Bang! Bang!" Two shots were heard and both ganders fell down dead among the reeds, and the water turned red from their blood.

"Bang! Bang!" Again came the sound of shots, and a flock of wild geese flew up.

The whole swamp was surrounded by hunters; from every direction came the awful noise. Some of the hunters had hidden behind bushes or among the reeds but others, screened from sight by the leaves, sat on the long, low branches of the trees that stretched out over the swamp. The blue smoke from the guns lay like a fog over the water and among the trees. Dogs came splashing through the marsh, and they bent and broke the reeds.

The poor little duckling was terrified. He was about to tuck his head under his wing, in order to hide, when he saw a big dog peering at him through the reeds. The dog's tongue hung out of its mouth and its eyes glistened evilly. It bared its teeth. Splash! It turned away without touching the duckling.

"Oh, thank God!" he sighed. "I am so ugly that even the dog doesn't want to bite me."

The little duckling lay as still as he could while the shots whistled through the reeds. Not until the middle of the afternoon did the shooting stop; but the poor little duckling was still so frightened that he waited several hours longer before taking his head out from under his wing. Then he ran as quickly as he could out of the swamp. Across the fields and the meadows he went, but a wind had come up and he found it hard to make his way against it.

Towards evening he came upon a poor little hut. It was so wretchedly crooked that it looked as if it couldn't make up its mind which way to fall and that was why it was still standing. The wind was blowing so hard that the poor little duckling had to sit down in order not to be blown away. Suddenly he noticed that the door was off its hinges, making a crack; and he squeezed himself through it and was inside.

An old woman lived in the hut with her cat and her hen. The cat was called Sonny and could both arch his back and purr. Oh yes, it could also make sparks if you rubbed its fur the wrong way. The hen had very short legs and that was why she was called Cluck Lowlegs. But she was good at laying eggs, and the old woman loved her as if she were her own child.

In the morning the hen and the cat discovered the duckling. The cat meowed and the hen clucked.

"What is going on?" asked the old woman, and looked around. She couldn't see very well, and when she found the duckling she thought it was a fat, full-grown duck. "What a fine catch!" she exclaimed. "Now we shall have duck eggs, unless it's a drake. We'll give it a try."

So the duckling was allowed to stay for three weeks on probation, but he laid no eggs. The cat was the master of the house and the hen the mistress. They always referred to themselves as "we and the world", for they thought that they were half the world — and the better half at that. The duckling thought that he should be allowed to have a different opinion, but the hen did not agree.

"Can you lay eggs?" she demanded.

"No," answered the duckling.

"Then keep your mouth shut."

And the cat asked, "Can you arch your back? Can you purr? Can you make sparks?"

"No."

"Well, in that case, you have no right to have an opinion when sensible people are talking."

The duckling was sitting in a corner and was in a bad mood. Suddenly he recalled how lovely it could be outside in the fresh air when the sun shone: a great longing to be floating in the water came over the duckling, and he could not help talking about it.

"What is the matter with you?" asked the hen as soon as she had heard what he had to say. "You have nothing to do, that's why you get ideas like that. Lay eggs or purr, and such notions will disappear."

"You have no idea how delightful it is to float in the water, and to dive down to the bottom of a lake and get your head wet," said the duckling.

"Yes, that certainly does sound amusing," said the hen. "You must have gone mad. Ask the cat — he is the most intelligent being I know — ask him whether he likes to swim or dive down to the bottom of a lake. Don't take my word for anything … Ask the old woman, who is the cleverest person in the world; ask her whether she likes to float and to get her head all wet."

"You don't understand me!" wailed the duckling.

"And if I don't understand you, who will? I hope you don't think that you are wiser than the cat or the old woman — not to mention myself. Don't give yourself airs! Thank your Creator for all He has done for you. Aren't you sitting in a warm room, where you can hear intelligent conversation that you could learn something from? While you, yourself, do nothing but say a lot of nonsense and aren't the least bit amusing! Believe me, that's the truth, and I am only telling it to you for your own good. That's how you recognize a true friend: it's someone who is willing to tell you the truth, no matter how unpleasant it is. Now get to work: lay some eggs, or learn to purr and arch your back."

"I think I'll go out into the wide world," replied the duckling.

"Go right ahead!" said the hen.

And the duckling left. He found a lake where he could float in the water and dive to the bottom. There were other ducks, but they ignored him because he was so ugly.

Autumn came and the leaves turned yellow and brown, then they fell from the trees. The wind caught them and made them dance. The clouds were heavy with hail and snow. A raven sat on a fence and screeched, "Ach! Ach!" because it was so cold. When just thinking of how cold it was is enough to make one shiver, what a terrible time the duckling must have had.

One evening just as the sun was setting gloriously, a flock of beautiful birds came out from among the rushes. Their feathers were so white that they glistened; and they had long, graceful necks. They were swans. They

made a very loud cry, then they spread their powerful wings. They were flying south to a warmer climate, where the lakes were not frozen in the winter. Higher and higher they circled. The ugly duckling turned round and round in the water like a wheel and stretched his neck up towards the sky; he felt a strange longing. He screeched so piercingly that he frightened himself.

Oh, he would never forget those beautiful birds, those happy birds. When they were out of sight the duckling dived down under the water to the bottom of the lake, and when he came up again he was beside himself. He did not know the name of those birds or where they were going, and yet he felt he loved them as he had never loved any other creatures. He did not envy them. It did not even occur to him to wish that he were so handsome himself. He would have been happy if the other ducks had let him stay in the henyard: that poor, ugly bird!

The weather grew colder and colder. The duckling had to swim round and round in the water, to keep just a little space for himself that wasn't frozen. Each night his hole became smaller and smaller. On all sides of him the ice creaked and groaned. The little duckling had to keep his feet constantly in motion so that the last bit of open water wouldn't become ice. At last he was too tired to swim any more. He sat still. The ice closed in around him and he was frozen fast.

Early the next morning a farmer saw him and with his clogs broke the ice to free the duckling. The man put the bird under his arm and took it home to his wife, who brought the duckling back to life.

The children wanted to play with him. But the duckling was afraid that they were going to hurt him, so he flapped his wings and flew right into the milk pail. From there he flew into a big bowl of butter and then into a barrel of flour. What a sight he was!

The farmer's wife yelled and chased him with a poker. The children laughed and almost fell on top of each other, trying to catch him; and how they screamed! Luckily for the duckling, the door was open. He got

out of the house and found a hiding place beneath some bushes, in the newly fallen snow; and there he lay so still, as though there were hardly any life left in him.

It would be too horrible to tell of all the hardship and suffering the duckling experienced that long winter. It is enough to know that he did survive. When again the sun shone warmly and the larks began to sing, the duckling was lying among the reeds in the swamp. Spring had come!

He spread out his wings to fly. How strong and powerful they were! Before he knew it, he was far from the swamp and flying above a beautiful garden. The apple trees were blooming and the lilac bushes stretched their flower-covered branches over the water of a winding canal. Everything was so beautiful: so fresh and green. Out of a forest of rushes came three swans. They ruffled their feathers and floated so lightly on the water. The ugly duckling recognized the birds and felt again that strange sadness come over him.

"I shall fly over to them, those royal birds! And they can hack me to death because I, who am so ugly, dare to approach them! What difference does it make? It is better to be killed by them than to be bitten by the other ducks, and pecked by the hens, and kicked by the girl who tends the henyard; or to suffer through the winter."

And he lighted on the water and swam towards the magnificent swans. When they saw him they ruffled their feathers and started to swim in his direction. They were coming to meet him.

"Kill me," whispered the poor creature, and bent his head humbly while he waited for death. But what was that he saw in the water? It was his own reflection; and he was no longer an awkward, clumsy, grey bird, so ungainly and so ugly. He was a swan!

It does not matter that one has been born in the henyard as long as one has lain in a swan's egg.

He was thankful that he had known so much want, and gone through so much suffering, for it made him appreciate his present happiness and the loveliness of everything about him all the more. The swans made a circle around him and caressed him with their beaks.

Some children came out into the garden. They had brought bread with them to feed the swans. The youngest child shouted, "Look, there's a new one!" All the children joyfully clapped their hands, and they ran to tell their parents.

Cake and bread were cast on the water for the swans. Everyone agreed that the new swan was the most beautiful of them all. The older swans bowed towards him.

He felt so shy that he hid his head beneath his wing. He was too happy, but not proud, for a kind heart can never be proud. He thought of the time when he had been mocked and persecuted. And now everyone said that he was the most beautiful of the most beautiful birds. And the lilac bushes stretched their branches right down to the water for him. The sun shone so warm and brightly. He ruffled his feathers and raised his slender neck, while out of the joy in his heart, he thought, "Such happiness I did not dream of when I was the ugly duckling."

The Twelve Dancing Princesses

The Brothers Grimm ~ Illustrated
by Errol Le Cain

THERE WAS ONCE a King who had twelve wonderfully beautiful daughters. They slept together in one great room, in twelve beds all in a row, and every evening the King locked them in. And yet every morning their shoes were worn out, as if they had danced all night.

The princesses would never admit that they had done anything but sleep peacefully in their beds, but the King was determined to find out the truth. He issued a proclamation announcing that anyone who could discover where the princesses danced at night should be allowed to choose one of them for his wife, and inherit the kingdom after the King's death. But he must find the answer within three days.

Very soon a prince arrived at the palace, offering to try to discover the secret. The King made him very welcome and when evening came he was shown to a chamber which opened off the great room where the princesses slept. There a splendid bed was waiting for him, and the door between the rooms was left ajar, so that the princesses could not steal away without his seeing them.

They all greeted him most politely and the eldest brought him a cup of wine. As he drank it, he thought how beautiful she was, and that was the last thought he had until the morning. Then he awoke and saw the princesses sleeping peacefully in their beds, and their worn-out shoes standing in a row. The same thing happened the next night and the night after that, and then the prince was dismissed from the palace, since he had failed in his task.

Many more princes followed him but they were all just as unsuccessful.

One day a poor soldier was limping along the high road that led to the King's palace. He had been wounded in battle and now he would never be able to fight again. On the way he met an old woman, who said, "Spare me a penny, kind sir."

"Here's a penny and welcome," said the soldier. "But it's all I can spare, for I've only six pennies left in the world."

"Where are you going then?" asked the old woman.

"I hardly know myself," said the soldier. "I suppose I must go to the city and beg my bread. That's what happens to old soldiers." But seeing the old woman look sad, he went on, "Don't worry about me, Grandmother. Perhaps I shall have a stroke of luck. Suppose I find out how the princesses wear out their shoes? Then I'll become King and have a wife into the bargain."

"That's not so difficult," said the old woman unexpectedly. "Only you must be sure not to drink the wine they offer you when you go to bed. Pretend to drink it and then pretend to fall asleep. Here, take this cloak." And she took a short, shabby cloak out of her bundle and handed it to

him. "It doesn't look much," she said. "But it will make you invisible. You can follow the princesses and find out where they go."

The soldier thought the old woman must be quite mad, but he didn't want to hurt her feelings, so he thanked her politely and took the cloak. He went towards the city, but after an hour or so the wind sprang up and he started shivering. "May as well put the cloak to some use," he said, "shabby as it is." He put it round his shoulders and stopped dead. He could no longer see himself.

"Merciful heavens," he said. "It's true." He took off the cloak again, wrapped it up carefully in his bundle, and went on towards the city.

"The old woman must have been a witch," he thought. "Or a good fairy. Perhaps I could really find out where the princesses go to dance."

So he went to the palace, and though he was so poor and shabby he was made as welcome as any prince. When night fell he was led to the bedchamber opening off the room where the princesses slept. They greeted him as politely as the other suitors and the eldest princess brought him a glass of wine. She smiled as she offered it to him, and he thought how beautiful she was, but he remembered what the old woman had said. He pretended to drink the wine but really he let it run down under his chin (and very sticky it felt). Then he lay down on the bed and pretended to snore.

The princesses laughed when they heard him, and then they took out their splendid gowns and dressed themselves for a ball. They were all in the highest spirits, except the youngest. "I don't know why it is," she said, "I feel so worried and miserable. I'm sure some terrible misfortune is going to happen."

"Don't be foolish, my darling," said the eldest princess. "Why are you always so timid? Remember how many princes have tried to guess our secret. This soldier, poor man, will be only too thankful for the chance of a good meal and a good sleep. He won't bother us."

All the same, she came to the open door between the two rooms and looked at the soldier, who kept his eyes shut and snored harder than ever. The princess seemed satisfied, and she went back to her bed and tapped it. At once it sank down through the floor, and a trapdoor appeared where the bed had stood. The eldest princess opened it and led the way down a long staircase into the darkness. The princesses followed her in turn, and the soldier sprang up, put on his cloak, and followed them. Because he was lame he found the stairs awkward, and once he stumbled and trod on the dress of the youngest princess, who was at the end of the line. She screamed and the line stopped.

"Someone trod on my dress," she cried, almost in tears.

"Don't be so foolish, my darling," said the eldest princess. "How could there be anyone behind you? You must have caught your dress on a nail."

The staircase went down and down and at last the soldier saw a gleam of light. It led into a marvellous silver forest where every leaf glittered and shimmered. "No one will believe this," thought the soldier, "I must have some evidence," and he broke off a silver twig.

The tree gave a loud crack and the youngest princess cried, "That sounded like a shot – what is wrong?"

"Nothing is wrong, my darling," said the eldest princess. "Our princes are firing a salute to welcome us."

They came to another forest where the trees were of gold and then to a third where they were made of diamonds. In each forest the soldier broke off a twig and each time the tree gave a crack and the youngest princess cried out in alarm. But the eldest repeated, "Our princes are firing salutes to welcome us."

As they came to the end of the diamond forest the soldier saw a lake and twelve little boats moored at the edge. In each boat sat a handsome prince and the princesses joined them, one to each boat. The soldier was still just behind the youngest princess, so he got in with her. The prince rowed away, but after a little while he said, "I can't think why the boat seems so heavy tonight."

"Everything is wrong tonight," said the youngest princess. "I feel so strange."

On the other side of the lake stood a splendid castle. Lights were blazing in every room, and drums and trumpets sounded a fanfare as the princes rowed their boats to the shore. They led the princesses into the castle's splendid ballroom, and there they danced and danced. The soldier amused himself by sometimes joining in the dance and giving one or other of the princesses an unexpected twirl, but they were too excited to notice, except for the youngest princess, who looked very upset whenever it happened to her. Once she left the dance and picked up a cup of wine, but the soldier took it out of her hand and drank it up. The

princess looked terrified, but her eldest sister came up and scolded her gently. "Don't be foolish, my darling. You imagined it."

They danced till two in the morning and by then their shoes were worn through. The princes rowed them back across the lake and this time the soldier got into the same boat as the eldest princess, and thought how beautiful she looked under the full moon.

At the edge of the diamond forest the princesses said goodbye and promised to come again the next night, and then they made their way sleepily back through the three forests. When they came to the stairs the soldier hurried on, so that he had time to take off his cloak and lie down on his bed before the princesses arrived. When they came in he snored loudly and the eldest princess laughed. "You see," she said, "we needn't trouble about him."

Then they put their worn-out shoes in a row and went to bed. Next day the soldier said nothing, for he wanted to see the forests and the castle and the dancing again and sit beside the eldest princess as they crossed the lake. That night and again the night after he followed the princesses and everything happened as before except that he did nothing to frighten the youngest princess, though she still looked anxious. The third evening the soldier took one of the jewelled cups from the castle and put it in his pocket, to be an extra proof of his story.

The next morning the King sent for him. "You have spent three days with us," he said. "Now I must ask you: where do my daughters dance at night?"

"Sire," said the soldier, "they dance with twelve princes in a castle underground."

He heard a rustle of skirts behind a curtain and he guessed that the princesses were listening.

"How can that be?" said the King.

Then the soldier described the trapdoor and the three forests and the lake and the castle.

"This is a very strange story," said the King. "Can you prove it?"

For answer the soldier took from his pocket the silver twig and the golden twig and the diamond twig and the jewelled cup.

The King looked at them for a long time and then he said, "Come here, my daughters." They came out from behind the curtain and stood in a row. They all hung their heads, except for the eldest princess, who looked thoughtfully at the soldier.

"Is this true?" said the King to the youngest princess, who burst into tears. Then he asked each of his daughters the same question and none of them answered until he came to the eldest princess.

She laughed and said, "The soldier has been too clever for us. Yes, Father, it is all true."

"He has been too clever for you," said the King, "and now he can marry whichever of you he chooses."

The soldier looked at the row of princesses. The youngest one was still crying and ten of her sisters looked indignant. But the eldest princess still looked thoughtful.

"I'm not as young as I was," said the soldier, "so I'll take the eldest."

At that the eldest princess burst out laughing. "There's a flattering reason," she said.

"It's a good reason," said the soldier. "You are the eldest and the cleverest and the most beautiful, and I've wanted to marry you ever since you gave me that sleeping draught."

"I believe a witch helped you," said the eldest princess.

"Or a good fairy," said the soldier.

The wedding was celebrated the same day with great splendor, the eleven younger princesses were bridesmaids, and the soldier and the eldest princess lived happily together all their lives.

The Sleeping Beauty

CHARLES PERRAULT ~ ILLUSTRATED BY JAN PANCHERI

Long long ago, in the days when the fairies were much more powerful than they are now, a King and Queen ruled over a far-off country. They dwelt in a splendid palace of marble, with costly carpets on the floor, beautiful paintings on the walls and ceilings, and dishes of gold on the tables, which were inlaid with jewels. They had hundreds of servants to wait on them, thousands of soldiers to guard them, and many wise men to help them rule their kingdom. But in spite of all of this, they were not happy. They had no child, and this grieved them very much.

One day the Queen was walking sadly by the river which would wind its way through the palace garden. As she strolled along, she saw a fish which had leaped out of the water to escape a cruel pike bent on catching it for his dinner. The poor thing was gasping for its life on the river-bank, and the kind-hearted Queen, feeling very sorry for it, picked it up and threw it back into the water. Imagine her surprise when the fish popped up its head and said: "You have been good to me, and I will tell you something which will make your heart rejoice. Your dearest wish shall be fulfilled. You shall have a little daughter."

The fish spoke the truth. A beautiful little daughter was born to the King and Queen and the parents were so happy that they tried to make every man, woman and child in the kingdom happy too. Great feasts were held in all parts of the country, but the grandest of all was held in the palace. All the lords and ladies were invited to the feast, and all the fairies too, except one who was left out by mistake. Before the banquet began the guests passed before the King and Queen and gave the baby princess all sorts of gifts. One of the fairies promised her goodness; another, beauty; a third, riches; and so on.

Then the great banquet was spread, and all the great folk of the land and all the fairies except one sat down to it.

In the midst of the gaiety there was a great hubbub outside, and suddenly the fairy who had not been invited burst into the banqueting chamber. She was angry as could be, and she said to the king and Queen: "You have not asked me to your feast, but I have come for all

that. I too, will give your daughter a gift — a gift that you will not like."

Then she laughed a wicked laugh that made everybody shudder.

"Listen," she said. "This is my gift. When the princess is fifteen years old she shall prick her finger with a spindle and fall down dead."

Thus saying, the thirteenth fairy laughed again and disappeared.

I don't think you can imagine the distress of the King and Queen when they heard what the wicked fairy had said. The poor Queen sobbed as if her heart would break, and the King could hardly keep back his tears. Just then a sweet, gentle voice was heard.

'I am the twelfth fairy," it said, "and I have not yet given my gift. I cannot undo the wickedness wrought by the bad fairy. This, however, I can do. When the spindle pricks the hand of the princess she shall not really die. She shall only fall asleep for a hundred years."

When the guests had departed, the King called all his wise men together and asked them how he was to prevent the evil which the thirteenth fairy had foretold. One of the wise men advised him that he should forbid all persons, on pain of death, to use a spinning wheel or keep a spindle in the house. This was done, and the King thought no harm could possibly come to his dearly loved child.

Time went by, and every year the princess grew sweeter in temper, more beautiful, more kindly and more helpful, so that every one loved her. At last her fifteenth birthday arrived.

Now on this very day the King and Queen were obliged to go on a journey to a distant part of the kingdom, and the princess was left behind in the palace. She roamed about from this chamber to that, and went to parts of the palace she had never visited before. At last she came to a flight of stairs, and at the top she found a little room in which an old lady sat spinning.

"What are you doing, good dame?" asked the princess.

"I am spinning," said the old lady, for she had not heard the King's proclamation.

"Please let me try," said the princess.

At once the old lady gave the spindle to the princess and she set the wheel in motion. Scarcely had she given the wheel one turn when the point of the spindle stuck into her finger. Down she fell and lay on the floor as if dead.

Strange to say, sleep fell upon every living thing in that palace at the same moment. The servants fell asleep on the roof; the dogs fell asleep in their kennels; even the fire on the hearth left off blazing and fell asleep too. The spit stopped turning, and the meat stopped roasting; the clocks stopped ticking. The trees round the palace stopped waving their branches and leaves. The cook went to sleep just as he was preparing the dinner, and the butler went to sleep just as he was lifting a jug of ale to his lips behind the pantry door. Everything and everybody stopped and slept. Even the King and Queen, who were sitting in the garden, fell asleep. As soon as the people in the palace were wrapped in slumber, a thick hedge grew up around it. Higher and higher it grew, until not even the tallest tower or the highest spire could be seen.

Long years passed away, and there was hardly a person alive who
remembered the story of the Sleeping Beauty. But one old man who
had been told the story by his father still remembered it. And he told
the tale to a young prince who had come to that land in search of
adventure.

"Behind yonder thicket of thorns," said the old man, "is a wondrous
palace in which a lovely princess, a King and Queen, and a household of
servants lie fast asleep. So have they slept for nigh a hundred years. Many
have tried to push their way through the thorns but none have
succeeded."

"I will try," said the prince, "and nothing shall hinder me."

A hundred years had now passed, and on that very day the prince set
off for the hidden palace. When he reached the thicket he set to work
with an axe, and after a few blows the hedge of thorns turned into a

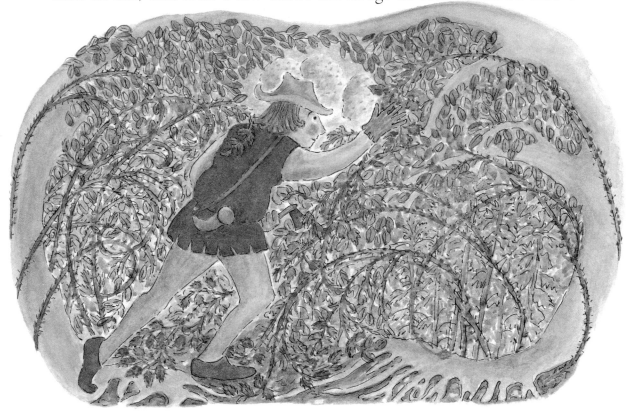

garden of beautiful flowers, which bent their stalks out of his way as he passed. In a few minutes he was at the palace gate. He passed the sleeping soldier at the portal; he saw the sleeping pigeons on the roof, the sleeping dogs in their kennels, the sleeping horses in the stables. Then he entered the palace and saw the sleeping servants, and noticed that even the flies slept on the walls. All were sleeping – it was a palace of sleep.

Through the silent halls the prince made his way. On and on he went until he reached a little room, and on a bed he saw fast asleep the most beautiful damsel that he had ever seen. Her eyes were closed, and her hair touched by the sunshine, lay like threads of gold on the snowy pillow. At once he fell in love with the beautiful princess and,

advancing to the bed, pressed a warm kiss on her cheek.

Instantly she awoke and smiled upon him. At that moment every living thing in the palace awoke too. The King and Queen awoke; the pigeons on the roof began to flutter their wings; the dogs in the kennels began to wag their tails; the horses in the stables began to neigh. The soldier at the gate began to walk up and down; the very flies on the walls began to buzz again. The fire in the kitchen blazed up once more; the spit began to turn, and the meat to roast. The cook went on preparing the dinner, and the butler behind the pantry door drank off his jugful of ale. Ah, what a glad awakening it was! Next day the princess and the prince were married, and I need not tell you that they lived happily ever after.

Hansel and Gretel

THE BROTHERS GRIMM ~ RETOLD BY NAOMI LEWIS
AND ILLUSTRATED BY LIDIA POSTMA

ONCE LONG AGO, at the edge of a great forest, there lived a poor
woodcutter with his wife and two children. The boy was called
Hansel, and the girl Gretel. Times were always hard for them, but then a
great famine seized the land and soon they had almost nothing to eat at
all. One night, as he tossed and turned, unable to sleep, the woodcutter
said to his wife, "What is to become of us? How can we feed our children
when there is scarcely a crust for ourselves?"

The wife said, "Listen, husband. Tomorrow we will take them deep
into the forest; we will light a fire for them and give them each a last piece

of bread. Then we will go back to our work. They'll never find their way home again, and we will have a better chance of surviving on our own!"

"I couldn't do that!" cried the poor father. "How can you think of leaving them alone in the woods? Why, they might be torn to pieces!"

"If they stay, we'll all die of hunger," said the wife. "You'd better start getting the coffin-wood now." And she gave him no peace until he stopped arguing, but he still didn't like the idea.

As it happened Hansel and Gretel had overheard everything that their parents had said. Gretel wept bitterly. "It's the end of us," she said.

"Sh," said the boy, "I'll find a way out, I promise you." And when at last the parents seemed asleep he crept out of bed, opened the lower half of the door and went outside. In the bright moonlight, the white pebbles all around the house shone like silver coins. The boy stuffed both of his pockets full and went back to his bed.

"Don't worry, Gretel," he said. "God will watch over us. And if He doesn't, I have something else that ought to keep us safe."

At dawn next morning, the mother shook the children awake. "Get up, you pair of lazybones," she said. "We are going into the forest to fetch wood." Then she gave them each a small piece of bread. "This is for your dinner," she told them. "But don't eat it all too soon, for there'll be no more today."

The family set out together. But then the father said, "Hansel, why do you keep looking back? You're keeping us waiting."

"Oh, I'm just waving goodbye to my white cat on the roof," said Hansel. "There he is, looking at me."

The woman said, "That's no cat; it's the sun shining on the chimney." But Hansel had really been making a trail of the white pebbles.

At last they came to the dark heart of the forest. "Now, children," said the woodcutter, "pile up some wood and I will light a fire to keep you warm."

Hansel and Gretel gathered the wood as their father instructed them.

When the little hill of brushwood had been lit, the mother said to them, "Lie down by the fire and rest for a bit. When we've gathered enough wood we'll come back for you."

The children huddled by the fire, and when midday came they ate their bits of bread. They thought they heard the blows of their father's axe; but the sound came from a branch which he had tied to a withered tree, blowing back and forth in the wind. Tired with waiting, the children fell asleep, and when they awoke it was night.

Gretel began to cry. "How shall we ever find our way home again?" she lamented.

"I told you not to worry," said Hansel. "Just wait until the moon rises, and you'll see." And when the moon was high in the sky, Hansel took his sister by the hand, and following his trail of pebbles, shining just like silver, led her home.

It was already dawn when they arrived. When the mother saw them at the door, she said, "You wicked children! Why did you sleep so long? We thought you were never coming!" But the woodcutter rejoiced to see them back.

For a while things went better. Then the famine started again, and the children overheard their mother say to their father, "All we have left is half a loaf of bread. After that, we'd better learn to eat wood. Those two will have to go. We'll take them further into the forest this time, and they'd better not try to get back."

The father felt wretched. "I would be happier sharing our last crumbs together," he said. But the woman persisted, until he gave in. If you've said yes once, it's hard to say no the next time. And so it was with him.

The children, though, were awake, and heard what was said. Hansel tried to go and gather pebbles as before, but the door was locked; there was no other way to get out. Gretel wept. "Quiet, Gretel," said the boy. "If there's a problem, then there must be an answer too."

Early next morning the mother roused the children from their bed. Again she gave them each a piece of bread, but smaller than before. Again, Hansel lagged behind the others and, as he walked along, he crumbled bits of bread and made a trail of breadcrumbs on the ground.

"Why are you lagging so?" said the father. "What are you looking back for?"

"My little pigeon on the roof is saying goodbye to me," said the boy.

"That's not a pigeon," said the mother, "that's the sun on the chimney." But Hansel went on scattering crumbs until the bread was gone.

Now, the woodcutter and his wife led Hansel and Gretel deep, deep into the forest, to a place they had never reached in all their lives before. Then once again the father built them a fire, and the mother said, "Stay here while we are out working, and if you feel tired take a nap. When we are finished, we will come and fetch you."

But hours crept by, and no one came. Gretel shared her piece of bread with Hansel, and then they fell asleep. When they awoke it was night.

"Don't worry, Gretel," said the boy. "When the moon rises, we'll be able to follow the trail of crumbs as we did before." But when the moon rose, there were no crumbs to be seen, for the birds had eaten them all.

"Oh, we'll find the way somehow," said Hansel. But they didn't. They walked the whole night and all the next day, and only got themselves deeper into the trees.

By now they were terribly hungry as well as tired and so they lay down and slept. When they woke up it was their third day in the wood. That afternoon they saw a beautiful, snow-white bird sitting on a bough. It sang so sweetly that they stood and listened. Then it flapped its wings, and flew on ahead of them, as if it wished them to follow. And follow they did, until it came to a tiny house, and settled on the roof.

The house was most unusual. It was made of bread; the roof was of rich iced cake, and the windows of sparkling sugar. "Well," said Hansel, "the Lord must have us in mind. You eat a piece of the window, Gretel. I'll take some of the roof." He reached up and broke off a piece of the roof, while Gretel leaned against the window and nibbled at the sweet delicious panes.

And then they heard a soft voice call, from inside:

> "*Nibble, nibble, mousekin!*
> *Who's nibbling at my housekin?*"

The children answered:

> "*The wind so wild,*
> *The Holy Child,*
> *Nothing more*
> *Is at your door.*"

But they were too hungry to stop eating. Hansel broke off a good chunk of the roof; Gretel took a whole round of window pane, and sat on the ground to enjoy it.

Suddenly, the door flew open and an old, old woman hobbled out. The children were so frightened that they dropped the cake and sugar. But the old woman simply said, "Oh, you dear little things, however did you get here? Come inside. There's nothing to be afraid of."

She grasped a hand of each and led them into the house. There she gave them a splendid supper of milk, pancakes and fruit, and when they could eat no more she tucked them into pretty little beds made with clean white linen. Hansel and Gretel thought they must be in heaven.

But they were wrong. The old woman was not being kind, oh no. She was a wicked witch whose favorite dish was roasted child. She had built her wondrous house just to lure them in. Witches, you know, have weak eyesight, but they also have a very keen sense of smell. This witch had known in advance that the two were on the way. "Here's a fine pair," she had told herself. "And they won't get away from me, oh no."

Early next morning she went up to look at them sleeping. "What tasty morsels!" she said. "But they'll do with a bit more fattening." She grabbed Hansel and locked him in a little stone prison with a window barred with iron. "Don't bother to scream," she said. "There's no one here to notice."

Then she poked at Gretel. "Get up, lazy thing," she said. "You must draw some water from the well and start cooking for your brother. I want him nice and fat."

When Gretel saw that her tears had no effect on the witch, she did as she was told. The best of food was now cooked for Hansel, and Gretel got nothing but crab shell. Every morning the witch would hobble over

to the shed and cry, "Hansel! Hansel! Stretch out your finger so that I can see how fat you're getting." But Hansel always held out a little bone instead.

"Why wasn't he getting fatter?" thought the witch, whose eyes were too dim to see the truth. But after four weeks, she decided to wait no longer. "Come, you," she called to Gretel. "Go and fetch some water, and no dawdling. I'm going to cook that boy, fat or thin."

Oh, how Gretel wept! "I wish we had died in the forest," she cried. "We'd at least have gone together."

"Oh, stop that blubbing, girl," snapped the witch. And early next day she told Gretel to light the oven fire while she herself made dough for the pie.

The oven was good and hot. "You get inside," said the witch, "and see if it's right for baking." She had just had the notion that Gretel might make an extra roasted dish. But Gretel guessed what the witch had in mind.

"I don't know how to get in," she said.

"Silly thing," said the witch. "You just creep through; the door is big enough. Look, I can get in myself," and she thrust her head inside to show her.

Quickly, Gretel gave a shove, slammed the door, and the witch was caught within. A foul smoke poured from the chimney along with the witch's screams.

The Princess on the Pea

HANS CHRISTIAN ANDERSEN ~ TRANSLATED BY STEPHEN CORRIN
AND ILLUSTRATED BY EDWARD ARDIZZONE

THERE WAS ONCE a prince who wanted to marry a princess, a *truly real* princess. So off he went travelling all over the world looking for one, but there was always something that wasn't *quite* right. For although there were lots and lots of princesses, the prince could never be absolutely certain whether they were *real* princesses or not; there was always something that didn't quite click. So back he came from his travels, very sad indeed, for he had so wanted to find a *real* princess.

One night there was a terrible storm – thunder and lightning and pouring rain – it was quite frightening. And in the middle of it all there was a violent knocking at the front door and the old King himself went to open it. And there outside stood a princess. But goodness me! What a sight she was, what with all that wind and rain! Water ran down her hair and clothes, trickling in through the toes of her shoes and out again at the heels. But she insisted she was a *real* princess!

"We can soon find out about that!" thought the old Queen, though she didn't actually say anything to the wet lady outside. She went up to the spare bedroom, removed all the bedclothes from the bed and put one pea on the bedstead. Then she got twenty mattresses, put them on top of the pea and then put a further twenty eiderdowns on top of the mattresses.

And in this bed the princess was to pass the night!

Next morning they asked her how she had slept.

"Oh, shockingly!" replied the princess. "I hardly slept a wink the whole night. I can't imagine what there was in the bed but it must have been something very hard because I'm black and blue all over. It was dreadful!"

Now they could see that she *was* a real princess because only a real princess would have felt the pea through twenty mattresses and twenty eiderdowns. No one except a real princess could be as tender-skinned as that.

So the prince married her, for now he knew for certain that she was a true princess. As for the pea, it was placed in a museum, and you can still see it there, unless someone has taken it away.

How about that for a true story!

Rumpelstiltskin

THE BROTHERS GRIMM ~ RETOLD BY ALISON SAGE
AND ILLUSTRATED BY GENNADY SPIRIN

THERE WAS ONCE a poor miller who never seemed to have any luck. No matter how hard he worked, he always seemed to grow poorer. At last he had nothing except his mill, his wife, and his beautiful daughter Rose.

"If the King thought you were somebody special," said his wife, "he would come to visit us. Then everyone would want to use our mill and we'd soon be rich."

"Don't be silly," said the miller, but his wife's words stuck in his mind and a daring plan came to him. Early the next morning he set off for the palace.

At the palace gates the miller asked to see the King. The King ordered the miller to be brought before him.

"Your Majesty," the miller began — and he trembled with fright as he spoke. "Your Majesty, my daughter can spin straw into gold."

"She can, can she?" said the King. "Bring her to the palace and we'll see. If what you say is true, then you'll be richly rewarded." He paused and frowned. "But if she fails, she'll lose her head."

This was not at all what the miller had expected.

"No, no … I made up the whole story!" he cried, but no one would listen. There was nothing left for him to do but go home and tell his daughter what the King had said.

Rose was horrified. "But what's done is done," she said. "The King may yet change his mind." And with that, she set out for the palace.

When the King saw lovely Rose, he was surprised at her grace and courage. But all he said was: "So here is our Goldenfingers! I have filled a room with straw for you. Before morning you must spin every scrap into gold — or lose your head."

Even the guards felt sorry for Rose as they locked her in the room at the top of the tower. How could anyone spin straw into gold?

Rose sat down by the spinning wheel and tears rolled down her cheeks.

"If there's one thing I hate, it's crying," said a voice at her elbow.

Startled, she looked down and saw a little man with a long grey beard.

"I beg your pardon," said Rose, "but who are you?"

"Never you mind," said the little man. "I know who *you* are and it would be a shame for you to lose that pretty little head. I might even help you, if you had something to give me in return."

Rose felt a sudden hope. "You can have my necklace," she said. "It belonged to my grandmother."

"Hmm, not much," said the little man, "but it'll do."

He sat down at the spinning wheel and — *whirr whirr whirr* — it went round so fast that all you could see was a blur and the flash of bright straw. Rose felt strangely sleepy as she watched him.

All of a sudden she heard the King opening the tower door. It was morning! Terrified, she leapt to her feet — and the room was full of glittering gold. Not one scrap of straw remained, and there was no sign of the little man.

The King was delighted but he did not show it. He wanted more gold.

"I have filled a second room with straw," he said. "If you spin every scrap into gold before sunrise, your father will have his reward. Otherwise, you'll lose your head."

Rose wept. This room was twice as big as the last one, but what did that matter? She could not spin even one piece of straw into gold.

"Still crying?" said a voice. It was the strange little man. "What will you give me this time to spin your straw into gold?"

Rose dried her tears as fast as she could. "My ring," she said. "It was given to me by my mother."

Exactly as before, the little man sat down at the spinning wheel and — *whirr whirr whirr* — exactly as before, Rose fell into a deep sleep. By the time the first rays of the morning sun slipped in through the tower window, the room was glistening with spun gold. But still the King wanted more.

"One more night you must spin straw into gold," he said. "If by sunrise not a scrap of straw remains, you shall become my wife. If you fail, you will lose your head."

He could not help hoping she would succeed. "Where else would I find a wife richer or more beautiful?" he thought.

Rose was locked in the tower for a third night, and the room was three times as big as before. Patiently she waited for the little man.

"What will you give me this time?" he asked as soon as he appeared.

"I have nothing left to give you," said Rose. "But if you take pity on me now, I'll give you anything you want when I am Queen."

"Anything, eh?" said the little man, his eyes glinting. "Then you must give me your firstborn child."

Poor Rose, what could she do but agree?

"Don't forget!" warned the little man. "We have made a bargain."

The King waited impatiently for the sun to rise. As he opened the door of the tower room, he blinked at the brilliance before him. The room was filled to the rafters with gleaming gold.

Soon all the bells in the land were ringing for the new Queen, and the miller and his wife cried with joy to see their daughter such a fine lady.

Many months passed – and by the time that Rose had a pretty little baby in her arms, she had forgotten all about the little man and her promise to him. But one day, almost a year later, she heard a horribly familiar voice at her elbow.

"We have a bargain, my lady," said the little man. "That child is mine!"

In vain Rose wept and offered him gold and jewels.

"What do I need with gold?" he grinned, his eyes as cold and bright as a lizard's. "But I cannot bear crying. Guess my name, and you can keep your child. I'll give you three days, and three guesses on each day. If you can't" – he tossed his grey beard impudently – "then the baby's mine!"

Rose quickly sent messengers

to ride to every corner of the land in search of names. First they found simple ones like Tom, Dick and Harry, James and John.

Then they brought in stranger ones like Wigglebottom and Curlytoes, Bundlewick and Chumpers. Rose's heart sank. How could she tell if any belonged to the little man?

At the end of the first day the little man appeared as promised.

"My name, lady?" he demanded.

"Is it Andrew?" she faltered.

"No!"

"Is it Belshazzar?"

"No!"

"Is it Caspar?" she said, almost in tears.

"No, and you'll never guess it," he crowed.

The second night Rose cried and begged, but the little man seemed to feel no pity. At each wrong guess his eyes lit up in triumph. "One more night and the baby is mine!" he jeered.

The third day came and Rose shut herself in her room. One more day, she thought, and my happiness is gone for ever. Out of her window she could see the King as he set off hunting.

When the King came home from hunting that evening, he went in search of his wife.

"Rose, my love," he said, "I've just heard the strangest thing. Such a funny, squeaky little song and you'll never guess who was singing it."

"No," said Rose, not lifting her head.

"A little man with a long grey beard."

"A long grey beard?" cried Rose.

"Yes," said the King, glad to see the success of his story. "And he was spinning almost as well as you can. I could hardly see the wheel, it went round so fast. Let me see, what was he singing?

> *"Nobody knows it*
> *Except him who chose it*
> *So I solemnly swear by the hair on my chin*
> *That my name it is: RUMPELSTILTSKIN!"*

Joyfully the Queen kissed her husband. She could hardly wait for the little man to arrive.

That evening he appeared as suddenly as ever.

"I'll save you the trouble and take the child now," he said gleefully. "You won't guess my name."

"Is it Alfred?" said Rose.

"Nooo!"

"Is it Archibald?"

"Certainly not!"

Then Rose pointed at him, laughing, and began to sing …

"Nobody knows it
Except him who chose it
So I solemnly swear by the hair on my chin
That my name it is: RUMPELSTILTSKIN!"

The little man froze, unable to believe his ears. Then he flew into a towering rage. "Some witch told you that!" he shrieked.

"Be off with you," said Rose. "I've kept our bargain!"

The little man was now in a hideous fury. He stamped his foot so hard that it went through the floor. He struggled to free himself, and his beard became tangled in the splintered wood. At last with a frightful scream he vanished, leaving nothing but a few wisps of grey hair behind.

That night Rose smiled happily as she sang her baby to sleep. She knew that as long as she lived, she would never again see Rumpelstiltskin.

Thumbelina

HANS CHRISTIAN ANDERSEN ~ RETOLD BY JAMES RIORDAN
AND ILLUSTRATED BY WAYNE ANDERSON

ONCE UPON A TIME there was an old widow who wished to have a child of her own. So she went to the wise woman of the village saying, "How I long for a little child. Can you help me?"

"Maybe I can, and maybe I cannot," replied the sage. "Take this magic barleycorn — it is not the kind that feeds the hens or grows in the fields — and plant it in a flowerpot. Then you shall see what you shall see."

"Thank you," said the widow, handing her a silver coin before hurrying home with the seed.

No sooner had she planted it than a tulip began to grow and bloom before her very eyes.

"What a pretty flower," she cried, kissing the petals. At once the tulip burst open with a pop. And in the very center of the flower sat a teeny tiny girl, neat and fair, and no bigger than the woman's thumb. So she called her Thumbelina.

The widow made a bed from a varnished walnut shell, a mattress out of violet leaves, and sheets from the petals of a rose. Here Thumbelina slept at night. In the daytime she played upon the table top. Sometimes

she would row a little boat from one side of the lake to the other. Her boat was, in truth, a tulip leaf; her oars, two stiff white horse's hairs; the lake, a bowl of water ringed with daisies. As she rowed, Thumbelina would raise her head and sing in a sweet, clear voice.

One night, however, while she lay sleeping in her cosy bed, a toad entered the room through a broken windowpane. It was big, wet and ugly, and it hopped upon the table where Thumbelina slept beneath her rose-petal sheet. When it saw the little child it croaked, "Here is the very wife for my son!"

Thereupon, it seized the walnut bed and hopped with it through the broken window and down into the garden.

Now, at the bottom of the garden flowed a stream; it was here, amidst the mud and the slime, that the toad lived with her son. And that son was more loathsome than his mother.

"Croak, croak, cro-o-ak," was all he said when he saw the little maid.

"Hush, you'll wake her," said the mother. "We won't be able to catch her if she runs away, she's as light as dandelion fluff. I'll put her on a water-lily leaf and that way she'll be safe while we make your home ready for the wedding."

Out in the stream grew a host of water lilies, their broad green leaves floating on the water. The mother toad set Thumbelina down on the leaf farthest from the bank. When the poor girl awoke the next day she found herself stranded and began to cry. There was no way she could reach the safety of the bank.

Meanwhile, the old mother toad was busy deep down in the mud decorating the wedding home with bulrushes and buttercups. When she had finished, she and her ugly son swam together to the water lily.

"This is my son, your husband to be. You'll be nice and snug down in the mud with him," she croaked. Then off they swam.

Thumbelina wept. She did not want to live with the toads, nor to have the slimy son for a husband.

The little fishes in the water now popped up their heads to peer at the tiny maid. When they saw how sad she was, they decided to help her escape. Crowding about the leaf's green stalk, they nibbled on the stem until the leaf broke free. Slowly it drifted down the stream, bearing Thumbelina to safety.

On and on sailed the leaf, taking Thumbelina on a journey she knew not where.

For a time a dainty butterfly hovered overhead, then finally settled on the leaf. Thumbelina was so glad to have company that she took the

ribbon from her waist and tied one end to the butterfly and one to the leaf. Now her boat fairly raced across the water, on and on and on. The radiant sun shone down upon the stream which glittered and glistened like liquid gold.

But Thumbelina's happiness was not to last. Presently, a large mayfly swooped down, seized her in its claws and flew up into a nearby tree. How frightened was poor Thumbelina as she soared through the air. Yet stronger than her fear was her sorrow for the butterfly; being still bound to the lily leaf it would be unable to feed itself and would surely die.

The mayfly, however, cared nothing for the butterfly. He set Thumbelina down upon the largest leaf, brought her honey from the flower pollen and sang her praises to the skies, even though she was nothing like a mayfly. By and by, all the mayflies that dwelt within the tree came to stare at the tiny girl. Two lady mayflies waggled their feelers in disgust, muttering scornfully, "But she has neither *wings* nor *feelers*. How ugly she is."

"Ugly, ugly, ugly," called all the mayflies in chorus.

The mayfly who had captured Thumbelina began to have his doubts; perhaps she really was as ugly as they said. Finally he made up his mind. He picked her up, carried her down to a daisy on the greenwood floor and left her there alone.

All through the summertime Thumbelina lived alone in the big wide wood. She wove herself a gossamer bed and hung it beneath a broad dock leaf, to shelter her from the rain. She ate honey from the flowers and drank dew each morning from their leaves.

Summer and autumn passed, and cold winter began its long reign. The birds that sang so sweetly flew away and the trees and flowers shed their blooms. Her dock-leaf canopy withered to a yellow stalk.

Thumbelina began to tremble with the cold, for her clothes were now quite threadbare. She was so frail and slender, poor little mite, that she would surely freeze to death. Snow began to fall. Each fluffy flake that fell upon her head was like an avalanche.

Thumbelina wrapped herself in a withered leaf, but it gave her little warmth and she shook and shivered with cold.

Now, close by the wood lay a cornfield. The harvest had long been taken in, leaving dry stubble standing stiffly in the earth. To the tiny maid, the corn stalks were like a great forest. It was here that Thumbelina came in search of shelter. All of a sudden she stumbled upon a little house. It belonged to a fieldmouse who lived there, warm and snug and with a well-stocked larder. Like a little beggar girl, Thumbelina knocked timidly at the door. "Little mouse, little mouse, please let me in," she cried. "I've had nothing to eat for these past two days."

"You poor little thing," said the mouse. "Come into my warm house and dine with me."

The fieldmouse soon took a liking to the child. "Stay here through the winter," she said. "You can keep my home clean and tell me fairy stories; I do so love a good story."

One day the fieldmouse announced, "We're going to have a visitor; my neighbor is coming to tea. He is rather a splendid fellow, with a rich velvet coat and a house much grander than mine. He would make you a fine husband. His sight isn't good, poor thing, so you'll have to tell him your finest stories." The neighbor was a mole.

Thumbelina was not at all keen to wed a mole.

Next day the mole arrived, dressed in his fine black velvet coat. True, he was clever and learned, but he hated the light; he hated the sunshine and flowers, even though he had never seen them.

After tea, Thumbelina was called upon to read and to sing. She sang so beautifully that the mole fell in love with her at once. But this he kept to himself.

Mole had recently dug a tunnel from the fieldmouse's house to his own, so that they could visit each other when they liked. "Don't be afraid of the dead bird lying in the passage," he said. "It has no sign of injury and has all its feathers and its beak. Goodness knows how it got into my tunnel. It must have died of cold."

The mole took up a piece of rotten wood to use as a torch and led them down the tunnel. Then he pushed his long nose up through the soil to make room for daylight.

There lay a swallow, its wings pressed close by its sides, its head and legs drawn beneath it as if sheltering from the cold. The poor thing was frozen stiff.

Thumbelina felt so sad, for she loved the birds that had sung sweetly to her all through the summer. But the mole merely kicked the bird, saying, "Serves it right for all its chattering. How awful to be born a bird. I'm glad none of my children will be birds. All they do is chirrup the livelong day, then die of hunger once winter comes." The fieldmouse agreed.

Thumbelina was silent. Yet when the mole and the mouse had turned their backs, she bent down and kissed the swallow's eyes. "Perhaps it was you who sang so sweetly to me," she thought.

That night Thumbelina could not sleep for thinking of the poor dead bird. At last she got up and wove a cover out of straw, carried it down the long dark passage and put it over the bird's still form. Then she fetched some blankets from the mouse's living room, putting them under the bird to protect it from the damp. "Farewell, pretty bird. And thank you for all your songs," she said. She pressed her head against the

above forests and lakes and snowy mountains. She shivered in the frosty air and snuggled deep inside the bird's warm feathers.

At last they reached the land where the sun's breath was warm, the heavens blue and the clouds high. In the orchards, trees bent low with oranges and limes, and the scent of myrtle and lavender filled the air. But still the swallow did not stop. On it flew until it came to a tree-fringed lake. On the banks were the ruins of an ancient palace where many birds had built their nests among the creepers and clinging fronds.

"Choose a flower growing down below," said the swallow, "and there I will leave you to make your home." Thumbelina clapped her tiny hands.

On the soft green grass below lay fallen pillars of stone, around which grew pale, pure lilies. The swallow set her down upon a leaf. Imagine the girl's surprise when she saw a young man sitting in the center of the flower. He was just as tiny, just as neatly formed and dainty as herself; yet he was wearing a pair of wings. "How lovely he is," said Thumbelina to the swallow.

"In every flower there dwells a youth or maiden," said the bird. "Each one is the spirit of the flower."

The young man looked at Thumbelina and thought her the loveliest creature he had ever seen. Taking her hand, he asked her to be his bride. Now here was a better husband than the loathsome toad or the mole in the velvet coat. Thumbelina readily agreed.

Right at that moment there appeared from every flower a tiny boy or girl, each bearing a gift. But the best gift of all was a pair of wings to enable her to fly.

"You shall have a new name," said the flower spirit. "From now on we will call you Maya."

"Farewell then, Maya," sang the swallow as he took flight.

Soon he would start his journey north to Denmark. It was there he had a nest, above the window of a storyteller – Hans Christian Andersen by name – who wrote down the tale related here.

The Frog Prince

The Brothers Grimm ~ Retold by Naomi Lewis
and Illustrated by Binette Schröder

ONCE, IN OLDEN TIMES, when wishes still had power, there lived a King. All of his daughters were beautiful, but the youngest was the loveliest of all. The sun itself, which sees so much, was dazzled when its light shone on her face.

Close to the King's castle was a great dark forest. In that forest, under an ancient lime tree, was a well.

Often, on hot summer days, the King's youngest daughter would wander into the forest and sit down on the edge of the cool well. Then, to pass the time, she would play with a golden ball, throwing it into the air and catching it again. She loved this toy; it was her special treasure. But one day she failed to catch the ball when it fell. It hit the ground, then bounced straight into the water.

The princess gazed down into the depths, but the ball had quite

disappeared. The well was so dark and deep that you could not tell what lay under the surface. She began to cry; her sobs grew louder and louder, filling the air with noise. She felt as if nothing could comfort her.

Suddenly she heard a voice. "Princess," it said, "whatever is the matter? Your howling would move the heart of a stone!"

Where did the voice come from? She looked round and saw a frog, poking his big ugly head out of the water. "So it was you speaking just now, old water-splasher! Why am I crying? I'll tell you. My golden ball fell down the well, and I've lost it now for ever."

"I can help you," said the frog. "But what will you give me if I bring back your plaything?"

"Whatever you want, dear frog," said the princess. "My finest clothes, my jewels, even my golden crown."

"Oh, I don't want clothes and jewels, things of that kind," said the frog. "But I *would* like some love and affection. Now if you promise to let me be your special friend and playmate, if you let me sit beside you at the dinner table, eat from your golden plate, drink from your golden cup, and sleep in your little bed — if you promise me all these small things I will dive down and bring back your golden ball."

"Yes, yes," said the princess, "I'll promise whatever you want if only you bring back my lovely ball." But she thought to herself: "The creature is talking nonsense. It's a frog! It lives in the water with frogs. How can it come to court and behave as if it were human?" The frog, though, heard only the promise. He nodded, then dived down into the well. After a while he swam to the surface with the golden ball in his mouth and shook it out on to the grass.

The princess was overjoyed to see her treasure again. She picked it up and rushed away. "Wait, wait!" cried the frog. "I can't run at that speed! Your legs are longer than mine." But his croaking calls were wasted. The princess raced on, reached the castle, and put the frog out of her mind. The poor fellow turned sadly and went back into the well.

The next day the princess sat down in her usual place at the royal dinner table. She was about to take a cherry from her golden plate when she heard a peculiar noise — *splosh, splosh, flop, flop* — on the marble stairs. Something was crawling up, step by step. That something reached the door and stopped. It knocked: *thud, thud*. It spoke in a croaking voice. "King's daughter," it said, "open the door!"

Fearfully the princess went to the door and peered outside. There was the frog, patiently waiting. She shut the door and quickly went back to her place at the table. Oh, she was afraid.

She sat quite still, but her heart beat fast — so fast that her father noticed. "Child," he said, "what is the matter? Is an ogre waiting outside to carry you off?"

"No, no," she said. "It isn't an ogre, it's a nasty frog."

"A frog? What does he want?"

"Dear Father, as I was playing by the well, my golden ball fell into the

water. I was crying so hard that the frog offered to bring it back. Only he made me promise to let him be my playmate and sit next to me at the table. I never thought that he could leave the well and come to the palace. Now he's outside and wants to come in!"

At that moment the knocking started again. *Thud, thud! Thud, thud!* and the listeners at the table heard these words:

> *"There was a princess*
> *Open the door!*
> *She made me a promise,*
> *I'll tell you more!*
> *A promise, a promise,*
> *That she must keep*
> *I've come for food and drink and sleep.*
> *Princess, O princess, you cannot hide!*
> *Your frog companion waits outside!"*

"Daughter," said the King. "You made a promise; it must be kept. Go and open the door."

Slowly the princess did as she was told. At once the frog hopped in and followed her footsteps to her chair. Then he called out, "Lift me up!"

"Do as he says," the King commanded.

But as soon as she had put the frog on the chair he leapt on to the table. "Move your golden plate nearer," he croaked, "and we can eat together."

The princess moved the plate, but it was easy to see that she was none too happy. The frog enjoyed the dinner — but what about the princess? Every morsel stuck in the poor girl's throat.

At last, the frog finished his meal and spoke again.

"I have eaten all I want," he said. "Now I am tired. Kindly carry me to your room, put me in your silken bed, and we can go to sleep."

The King's daughter began to cry. She was really afraid of the frog, so cold to the touch — and now he wanted to sleep in her beautiful clean bed.

But the King frowned, and said sternly, "If someone has helped you in time of need, you must not scorn him when the need has gone."

What could she do? She picked up the frog between finger and thumb, carried him upstairs and put him down in a corner.

She waited a little while, then went to bed.

But no sooner was her head on the pillow than she heard the frog creeping along the floor. "I am tired," he said. "I want to sleep comfortably, just as you do. Now pick me up, or I shall tell your father."

The princess was enraged, but she dared not refuse. She picked up the frog and then — with a rush of anger — threw him with all her might against the wall.

As she did so, she cried out: "Now are you satisfied, you nasty creature?"

But even while he fell, an astonishing thing happened. The frog began to change his shape; he was a frog no longer, but a young and handsome prince, gazing at her with eyes that were both beautiful and kind.

The King rejoiced at the news. He welcomed the prince as a husband for his dear daughter, and so the two were married. The prince had a strange tale to tell. A wicked witch had cast a spell on him, a spell that only the loveliest princess could break. Now he was free! "Tomorrow," he said, "we shall travel to my kingdom." Then they fell asleep.

When morning came they were wakened by the sun. They saw that a carriage was waiting at the gates. It was drawn by eight white horses with ostrich plumes on their heads and trappings all of gold. At the back stood a serving man with three iron bands around his heart. So great had

been the man's grief when his master was
bewitched that he had placed the three bands
around him to keep his heart from breaking.

"My faithful Henry!" said the prince, and
greeted him joyfully.

And now the bride and bridegroom were
ready to leave for the young man's own
kingdom. Faithful Henry lifted each one into
the carriage, then took his place
behind them.

After they had driven a short
distance a sharp crack was heard.

Startled, the bridegroom
spoke:

"Henry, Henry, what's that sound?
Is the carriage breaking?
No, Sire, 'tis a ring that bound
My heart when it was aching.
But now my lord is freed and back,
Joy has made the iron crack."

Then a second time they heard a crack, and a third time after that. Each time the prince feared that the carriage was breaking. But no — the sound came from the last of the bands freeing faithful Henry's heart.

"Grief forged the bonds at first:
Grief for his lord accurst.
Joy made the bonds to burst."

Rapunzel

THE BROTHERS GRIMM ~ RETOLD AND
ILLUSTRATED BY JUTTA ASH

ONCE UPON A TIME, there lived a man and his wife; the one thing they lacked was a child. Now at the top of their house was a little room with a window which looked out over a beautiful walled garden. In it grew the loveliest flowers and the most luscious fruit and vegetables. But the wall around was high; what's more, the garden belonged to a witch!

One day, the wife noticed a bed planted with a special kind of fresh green lettuce known as rapunzel. How she longed to taste it! Very soon, she could think of nothing else. Day by day she grew paler and thinner, until she had dwindled into a shadow of herself, for no other food could tempt her, nothing at all.

Her husband was alarmed to see her fading away.

"Wife, wife," he said. "What is troubling you?"

"It's the rapunzel in that garden," she replied. "I shall die unless I have some to eat."

"What's to be done?" thought the good man. "If she must have it, she must, witch or no witch." So, that very evening, he scrambled over the high

184

wall, stealthily pulled up a bunch and brought it back to his wife. Oh, she was overjoyed! She made it into a salad and — crunch, crunch, how delicious! — in a minute there wasn't a shred left. Next day, she craved for that green stuff even more; there was nothing else she would eat.

What could the husband do? Again, he waited until dusk and climbed into the magic garden. He bent down to pick a quick handful of the rapunzel, but what a fright awaited him! There, standing over him, was the witch herself, wild with rage. "Thief!" she cried. "You'll regret it!"

"Forgive me," begged the poor man, and he told her of his wife's great longing for the leaves. The witch grew calmer as she listened.

"Very well," she said at last. "You may take as much as you need, but on one condition. As soon as your wife has a child, you must give that child to me. It will be well looked after, I promise you."

Well, the man was so relieved that the witch had not worked some dreadful spell on him that he quickly agreed to the bargain. Sure enough, when the wife gave birth to a beautiful baby girl soon afterwards, the witch arrived promptly to claim her debt. "Rapunzel shall be her name!" she declared, and she carried the child away.

What a beautiful girl she grew to be! But when she was twelve years old the witch shut her up in a high tower, far away in a wood. The tower had neither door nor staircase, only a tiny window right at the top. Whenever the witch came to visit her charge, she would call up to the window:

> *"Rapunzel, Rapunzel,*
> *Let down your golden hair!"*

For Rapunzel had wonderful long golden hair which she often wore in thick plaits. Each time she heard the witch's call she would wind the plaits round the hook on the window ledge and let them fall all the way down to the ground. The witch would then seize hold and climb up until she reached the window.

Some years passed, and one day a young prince was riding through the wood. He heard the sound of sweet singing, followed the voice and found himself at the foot of a tall tower. But where was the door? Who was the singer? Whoever it was, the voice was so enchanting that the prince came day after day to listen.

One evening, from his hiding place behind a tree, the prince saw a strange woman emerge from the wood and stand at the foot of the tower. There she called these words:

> *"Rapunzel, Rapunzel,*
> *Let down your golden hair!"*

At once a great length of golden hair slid to the ground, and the woman hauled herself up to the window.

"Aha!" thought the prince. "A ladder for one is a ladder for another!" So the next evening he too stood at the foot of the tower and called up:

> *"Rapunzel, Rapunzel,*
> *Let down your golden hair!"*

Immediately the shining hair fell to his feet, and the prince climbed up and up until he reached the window at the top.

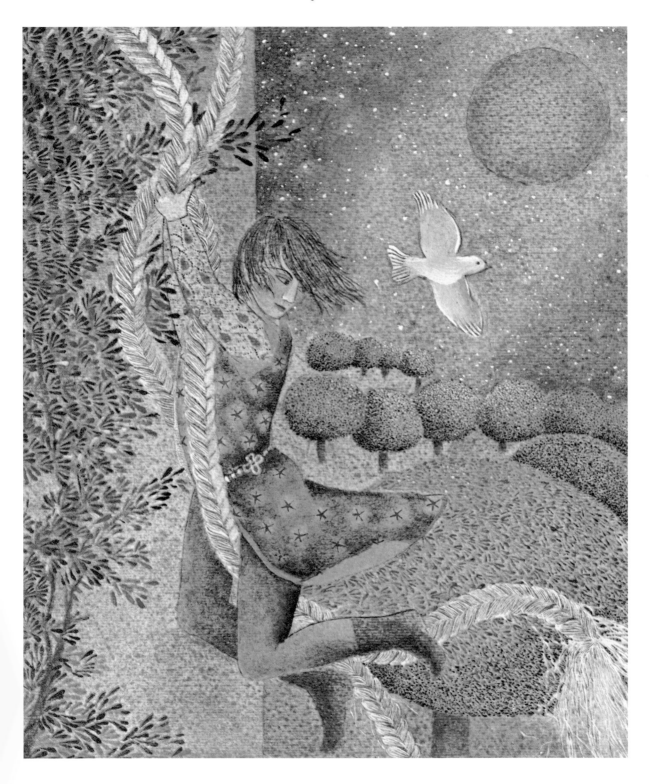

At first Rapunzel was alarmed when the prince appeared, for she had never seen anyone before but the witch. But he talked to her so kindly that she soon lost her fear. "Your singing brought me here," said the prince. "I listened so often." And he begged her to escape and be his wife.

"I would come gladly," said Rapunzel, "but how can it be done?"

At last they thought of a plan. Every night the prince would bring a skein of silk. Rapunzel would weave this into a ladder; when it was long enough to reach the ground, she would climb down into freedom, and away they would ride together.

Each night the silken ladder grew longer; each day Rapunzel hid it well. But one day she made such a bad mistake! "Tell me, Mother," she said. "Why do you climb so slowly up to the window? The prince is here quick as lightning." Oh — what had she said! The witch was in a frenzy.

"So you've had a visitor!" she hissed. "I thought I had kept you away from the world, but you have deceived me. Well, there's an answer to that." She snatched up a pair of scissors, grasped the thick hair in her other hand, and — snip! snap! — the golden tresses fell and covered the floor. Then the witch-woman dragged the poor girl off to a forest wilderness, and left her there to live on berries and nuts as well as she could.

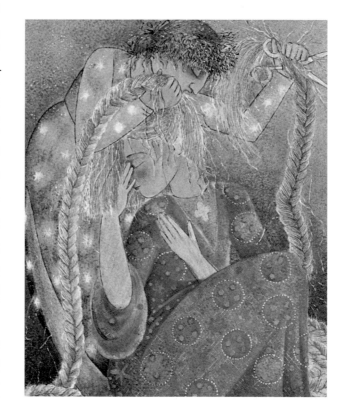

Back in the tower the witch picked up the severed hair and wound it round the hook. She did not have to wait long. Far down below came the call:

"Rapunzel, Rapunzel,
Let down your golden hair!"

The golden hair came down; the prince climbed up — but imagine his horror when the window came into view! There he beheld not the lovely Rapunzel but the mocking face of the witch. "Ha!" she cried. "So you've come for my daughter! But you are too late — the bird has flown. You'll never see her again." She burst into peals of laughter — and the prince, maddened by shock and despair, leapt from the window to the ground.

Down … down …

He was not killed, for a great bush of thorns broke his fall. But the thorns pierced his eyes and made him blind. Sadly he wandered hither and thither, through the land, through the forest, thinking only of the beautiful girl who should have become his bride.

Many days had come and gone when the prince by chance reached the wilderness which was now Rapunzel's home. There she lived

meagerly with the little twins, boy and girl, who had been born to her in the forest. Suddenly he stopped. That voice, that singing — whose could it be but Rapunzel's? He moved towards the sound. Rapunzel saw him and twined her arms round him, tears running down her face. Two of the tears fell on the prince's eyes — wonderful! He could see! So they made their joyful return to his kingdom, where they lived happily ever after.

Snow White

THE BROTHERS GRIMM ~ RETOLD BY
NAOMI LEWIS AND ILLUSTRATED BY
LIDIA POSTMA

ONCE LONG AGO, in the middle of winter, when snowflakes drifted down from the sky like feathers, a Queen sat sewing by a window which was framed with ebony. As she looked up from her sewing to gaze at the falling flakes, she pricked her finger with the needle, and three drops of blood fell down on to the snow. The red drops looked so beautiful on the snow that she said to herself, "Ah, if only I had a child who was as white as snow, as red as blood and as black as the wood of this window-frame!"

Soon after that, the Queen gave birth to a daughter whose skin was as white as snow, whose lips were as red as blood, and whose hair was as black as ebony, and the little princess was called Snow White. But when the child was born, the Queen died.

A year passed, and the King took another wife. She was a beautiful woman, but proud and haughty, and couldn't endure the thought that anyone else might be more beautiful than she. Every day she would stand before her magic mirror, saying,

> *"Mirror, mirror, on the wall,*
> *Who is the fairest one of all?"*

And every day the mirror would answer,

> *"Queen, Queen, fair Queen,*
> *In me the truth is seen.*
> *Rival beauty is there none —*
> *You are still the fairest one."*

This made the Queen feel content, since she knew that the mirror had to speak the truth.

But as Snow White grew, so did her beauty. By the time she was seven years old, she was as beautiful as the day, more beautiful even than the Queen herself.

One morning, when the Queen asked,

> *"Mirror, mirror, on the wall,*
> *Who is the fairest one of all?"*

the mirror answered,

> *"You are as fair as fair can be,*
> *But young Snow White is more fair than thee."*

The Queen turned yellow and green with rage and fury, and from that hour on, whenever she saw Snow White, her hatred made her heart turn over within her.

Her pride and envy grew and grew and gripped her heart like weeds; she could think of nothing else. At last, she sent for a huntsman. "Take that child into the forest and get rid of her," she said. "And bring me back her lungs and liver so that I know you've done it."

The hunter set off with the little princess, but when he reached the woods and drew his knife, the girl began to weep. "Good huntsman, let me live," she begged. "I'll run off into the forest and never come back, I promise you."

Because she was so beautiful, the huntsman took pity on her. "All right, you poor little thing, run away," he said, and he thought to himself, "Well, the wild beasts will probably deal with her."

Then a young boar appeared. The huntsman killed it, cut out its lungs and liver and took them to the Queen as proof that the girl was

dead. The Queen was delighted. She ordered the cook to salt and stew these entrails, and ate them for her dinner, thinking that they came from the dead Snow White.

Snow White was alive, however, but she was all alone in the great forest, with its rustling leaves and darkness, and she wept with terror because she didn't know what to do. She began to run hither and thither, paying no attention to the sharp stones underfoot and the tearing thorns and brambles; the wild beasts saw her pass but did nothing to harm her. She ran and ran till her legs would scarcely carry her and then, when the day had almost gone, she came to a little house.

Everything in the house was tiny, but as neat and clean as could be. There was a tiny table covered with a white cloth, and on the table were

"She is the most beautiful girl I have ever seen. Let me have the coffin, and I will give you whatever you ask."

But there was nothing that the dwarfs wanted. "We will not part with her for all the gold in the world," they said.

"Then let me have it as a gift," said the prince, "for I cannot live without seeing Snow White. I will honor and love her as though she were still alive."

The dwarfs took pity on him and let him take the coffin. But as the prince's men were carrying it away on their shoulders, they stumbled over a tree stump, and the jolting shook the coffin so much that the piece of poisoned apple came out of Snow White's throat. She opened her eyes and sat up with a cry. "Where am I?" she asked.

"You are with me," said the prince. Then he told her all that had happened. "I love you more than anything in the world," he said. "Come with me to my father's castle and be my wife."

Snow White went with him, for she loved him too, and wedding celebrations of great magnificence were announced through the land.

Now one of the guests invited was the wicked Queen. Before she left, dressed in her most beautiful clothes, she stood as usual before the mirror, saying,

> *"Mirror, mirror, on the wall,*
> *Who is the fairest one of all?"*

And the mirror answered,

> *"O Queen, fair Queen,*
> *In me the truth is seen.*
> *No one is as fair as you,*
> *Except Snow White, a Queen now too."*

The Queen was so struck with horror that she didn't know what to do next. But at last her curiosity got the better of her and she decided to go to the wedding to see the bride for herself. The moment she entered the ball she recognized Snow White. But she could not escape. Red hot iron shoes were put on her feet, and she was made to dance until she fell down dead.

Long Ago and Far Away

The Wild Swans

HANS CHRISTIAN ANDERSEN ~ RETOLD BY NAOMI LEWIS
AND ILLUSTRATED BY ANGELA BARRETT

FAR, FAR AWAY, in the land where the swallows fly during our winter, there lived a King who had eleven sons and one daughter, Elisa. The eleven brothers — princes all of them — went to school, each wearing a star at his heart and a sword at his side. They wrote on leaves of gold with diamond pencils; whatever they read, they learned at once. You could tell straight off that they were princes! Their sister Elisa sat on a little stool made of looking-glass, and had a picture book that had cost half a kingdom.

Oh, they lived royally, those children! But it did not last. The King, their father, married an evil Queen, and she didn't care for the children at all. They realized this on the very first day. A great celebration was held to welcome her, and the children, too, decided to play at guests-for-tea. But instead of the cakes and roasted apples which they were usually given, the Queen allowed them only a cupful of sand. They would have to pretend that it was cakes and apples, she told them.

A week later, she sent off little Elisa into the country, to live with a peasant family. And it wasn't long before she had filled the King's head with such shocking tales about the poor young princes that he wished to have nothing more to do with them.

"Out you go!" said the wicked Queen to the boys. "Fend for yourselves as you may. Fly off as voiceless birds!"

Yet she could not do as much harm as she wished, for they turned into eleven beautiful wild swans. With a strange cry, they flew out of the palace windows, over the fields and forests, far away.

Early in the morning when they passed the place where their sister Elisa had been sent, they circled about the cottage roof, flapping their wings and craning their necks. But nobody heard or saw. At last they had to fly on, upwards into the clouds, out into the wide world.

Poor little Elisa sat in the cottage playing with a green leaf, the only toy she had. She pricked a hole in it and peeped through at the sun. The brightness seemed like the bright eyes of her brothers.

Time passed, one day just like another. But whenever the wind blew through the garden, it whispered to the roses: "Who could be more beautiful than you?" And the roses would answer: "Elisa is more beautiful." What they said was the truth.

When Elisa was fifteen she was brought back to the palace. The evil Queen, seeing how beautiful she was, was very vexed indeed. She would have promptly turned her into another wild swan like her brothers, but she did not dare just yet, for the King had asked to see his daughter.

Early next morning, the Queen went into the bathroom with three toads. She kissed the first and said, "Hop on to Elisa's head, and make her as slow and dull as you." Kissing the second, she said, "Make her look just like you so that her father will not know her." Then she kissed the third toad, whispering, "Fill her with evil, so that she knows no peace."

She put the toads into the clear water, which at once took on a strange greenish tinge. Yet Elisa seemed not to notice them. And when she rose from the water, they were gone; but three scarlet poppies were floating there. If the toads had not been poisoned by the kiss of the wicked Queen, they would have become red roses. But flowers they had become from Elisa's touch alone.

When the Queen perceived how she had failed, she rubbed Elisa's skin with dark brown walnut juice and made her hair look wild and tangled. You wouldn't have recognized her!

And so, when her father saw her, he was shocked. "That is not my daughter!" he declared. No one else at court would have anything to do with her except the watchdog and the swallows and who ever bothered about what *they* thought?

Poor Elisa started to cry. She crept out of the palace, and walked all day through field and moor and meadow, until she reached a great dark forest, leading to the sea. She had no idea where she was but she fixed her mind on her brothers. They had been driven forth like herself, and now she would go to the ends of the earth to find them.

Night fell, and she lay down on the moss. All was silent; the air was mild and touched with a greenish light — it came from hundreds of glow-worms. There were so many that when she gently touched a branch, a shower of the shining creatures dropped down like stars.

All that night she dreamt about her brothers. They were playing together, as they did when they were children, writing with the diamond pencils on the leaves of gold, looking at the beautiful picture book that had cost half a kingdom. Only now they were setting down all that had befallen them, bold deeds and strange adventures. Everything in the picture book seemed to come alive; the birds sang, the people stepped out of the pages and spoke to her. But when she turned over a page they jumped straight back, so as not to get into the wrong picture.

When she awoke the sun was high overhead, though she could hardly see through the thick leaves and branches of the trees. But where the sunbeams shimmered through the moving leaves there was a dancing golden haze. The air was filled with the smell of fresh green grass; the birds flew so near that they seemed about to perch on her shoulder. She

heard the splashing of water; it came from a spring which flowed into a pool, so clear that you could see the sandy bed below.

But when Elisa saw her own face in the water, she was startled — it was so grimy and strange. She dipped her hand into the pool and rubbed her eyes and forehead — what a contrast! Her own clear skin shone through. She took off her clothes and stepped into the fresh cool water — and a more beautiful princess could not have been found anywhere in the world.

As she set off again, she met an old woman who gave her some berries from a basket that she was carrying. Elisa asked her if she had come across eleven princes riding through the forest.

"No," said the old woman. "But yesterday I saw eleven swans with golden crowns on their heads swimming down yonder river." Elisa thanked her and walked along the winding water until it reached the sea. There the great ocean lay before her. What was she to do?

Then she saw, scattered about the seagrass, eleven swan feathers. She looked up; eleven wild swans were flying towards the land, like a long white ribbon. Each had a golden crown on its head. Flapping their great wings, they landed near her.

A moment later the sun sank below the water; the swans seemed to shed their feathery covering — and there stood eleven handsome princes. Elisa ran forward and threw herself into their arms, calling them each by name. They in turn were overjoyed to see their little sister, and they told her their strange tale.

"We brothers," said the oldest, "have to fly as swans so long as the sun is in the sky. When night has come we return to human shape; that is why we must look for a landing place well before sunset. If we were flying high in the air when darkness came, we should hurtle down as humans to our deaths.

"We do not dwell here any more. Our home is now a land far across the sea. To reach it we have to cross the vast ocean — and there is no island where we can rest in our human form during the night. Only one thing saves us. About halfway across, a little rock rises out of the water — just large enough to hold us standing close together. If it were not there, we would never be able to visit our native land again, since we need the two longest days of the year for our flight. Once a year we fly over this mighty forest, and gaze at the palace where we were born, and circle over the tower of the church where our mother is buried.

"The wild horses gallop across the plains as they did in our childhood; the charcoal-burner still sings the old songs that we danced to as children. Here is our native ground, the place that will always draw us back. But tomorrow we must set off again for that other land, and we cannot return for another year. Have you the courage to come with us, little sister?"

"Oh, take me with you," Elisa said.

All that night they set about weaving a net of willow bark and rushes. When the sun rose and the brothers turned into swans, they picked up the nets with their beaks, and flew with Elisa into the clouds. One hovered just overhead to shade her from the sun's hot rays.

Now they had reached such a height that the first ship they saw looked like a seagull resting on the water. A great cloud lay behind them, a mountain of cloud, and on it Elisa saw the shadows of herself and her brothers. They were like giants' shadows, vast and wonderful. But the sun rose higher and cloud and shadow pictures disappeared.

All the long day they flew, like arrows across the sky. Yet, swift as they were, they were slower than at other times, for they now had their sister to carry. Night was near, the air was full of thunder, but there was still no sign of the tiny rock. Elisa looked down with terror. At any moment now her brothers would change to humans and all would fall to their deaths. Black clouds surrounded them; storm winds churned the leaden water; flash after flash of lightning pierced the gloom.

Suddenly, the birds headed downwards. The sun was already halfway into the sea – but now, for the first time, she saw the little rock; it could have been a seal's head looking out of the water. Then her feet touched the ground, and at that moment the sun went out like the last spark on a piece of burning paper. All round her stood her brothers, humans now, sheltering her from the dashing waves.

At dawn the air was clear and still. The sun rose; the eleven swans soared from the rock, with Elisa on her airy raft, and went on with their journey. From far above, the white foam on the dark

green waves looked like thousands of floating swans.

Then Elisa looked ahead, and beheld a range of mountains, with glittering icy peaks; in their midst was a mighty palace, at least a mile in length. Below were groves of waving palm trees, and wonderful flowers, vast in size, like mill-wheels. Yet all this seemed suspended in the air. Was it the land they were making for? But the swans shook their heads. What she was seeing, they told her, was the cloud palace of the fairy Morgana, lovely but ever-changing; no mortal might enter there.

And as Elisa gazed, mountains, palace, trees and flowers all dissolved, and in their place rose a score of noble churches, with lofty towers. She thought that she heard organ music — or was it the sound of the sea? Then, when they seemed quite near, the churches changed to a fleet of ships sailing just below. She looked again — there were no ships; all she saw was a whirl of mist over the water. Sea and air and sky are ever in motion, ever changing; no vision comes to the watcher twice.

And then Elisa glimpsed land at last. Blue mountains of rare beauty rose up before her; she could just discern forests of cedar, cities and palaces. The swans came down, and Elisa found herself at the mouth of a hillside cave; an opening almost hidden by a web of vines and other delicate greenery. "You can sleep here safely," the youngest brother said.

Was it a dream? She thought that she was flying through the air, straight to the cloud-castle of the fairy Morgana. The fairy herself came to meet her. She was radiant and beautiful — but she was also very much like the old woman who had given her berries in the forest, and had told her of the swans with golden crowns.

"Your brothers *can* be freed," said the fairy. "But it will take no ordinary courage. Look at this stinging nettle. It grows plentifully round the cave where you are now sleeping — and in only one other place: on churchyard graves. Now, first you must gather them yourself, though they will sting and burn your skin. Then you must tread on them with bare feet until they are like flax. This you must twist into thread and weave into cloth; from it you must make eleven shirts like coats of mail with sleeves. Throw one of these over each of your brothers and the spell will break. But – this is important – until you finish your task, even if it takes years, you must not speak. A single word will pierce your brothers' hearts like a knife. Their lives depend on your silence. Remember!"

She touched Elisa's hand with the nettle. It scorched her skin like fire, and she awoke. It was bright daylight; nearby lay a nettle like the one she had seen in her dream. Elisa went outside the cave – yes, there the nettles were! She would start at once. She plucked an armful, trampled them with bare feet, and began to twist the green flax into thread.

At sunset her brothers returned. At first her silence alarmed them. But then they guessed that she must be doing this strange work for their sakes.

All that night she worked. When day returned, the swan-brothers flew far afield, and she sat alone, but never did time go so fast. One shirt was already finished, and she started on the next.

All at once, a sound rang through the mountains – the sound of a

distant hunting horn. She heard the barking of dogs and she was seized with terror.

Then a great hound sprang out of the bushes. It was followed at once by another, then another; they made for the mouth of the cave. Before many minutes, all the huntsmen had gathered at her hiding place, and the most handsome of all stepped forward. He was the King of that land. He saw Elisa, and she seemed to him the most beautiful girl in the world.

"How do you come to be here?" he asked. Elisa shook her head; she dared not speak. "Come with me," said the King. "If you are as good as you are beautiful, you shall wear a gold crown on your head, and the finest of my castles shall be your home."

He lifted her on to his horse and they galloped off through the mountains. His companions rode behind.

They reached the royal city at day's end. The King led Elisa into his palace, where sparkling fountains splashed into marble pools and the lofty walls and ceilings were covered with marvellous paintings. But she wept and grieved and saw nothing. Listless and pale, she let the women dress her in royal robes, twine her hair with pearls and cover her damaged hands with gloves.

And so at last she entered the great hall. She was so dazzlingly beautiful that all the court bowed low before her and the King announced that she would be his bride. But the archbishop shook his head and whispered that the wood maiden from the forest must surely be a sorceress who had cast a spell on his heart.

Yet the King would not hear a word against her. He ordered the music to strike up and the rarest dishes to be served; she was taken through fragrant gardens and splendid halls. But nothing touched her grief. Then the King showed her a little room which would be her own. Carpeted in green, hung with costly green tapestries, it was made to look like the cave where she had been found. On the floor lay the bundle of nettles and flax; from the ceiling hung the one shirt that she had finished. A huntsman had brought these things along as a curiosity.

"Here you can dream yourself back in your old home," said the King. "Now when you wish, you can amuse yourself by thinking of that bygone time."

When Elisa saw what was so near to her heart, a smile came to her lips, colour returned to her face and she kissed the King's hand. He took her in his arms and gave commands for all the church bells to be rung for their wedding. The lovely mute girl from the forest would be Queen.

Then came the wedding day. The archbishop himself had to place the crown on Elisa's head, and he pressed it down so spitefully that it hurt. But she felt a deep affection for the good and handsome King and day by day, she loved him more and more. If only she could speak! But first, she had to complete her task. So each night, as the King slept, she would steal from his side, and go to her work in the room like a green cave. Six shirts were now complete. But she had no more flax. And only in the churchyard could she find the right nettles.

So at midnight, full of fear, she crept down through the moonlit garden, along the great avenues, and out into the lonely streets that led to the churchyard. What a sight met her eyes! A ring of lamias, those witches that are half snake, half woman, sat round the largest gravestone. Elisa had to pass close by them, and they fastened their dreadful gaze upon her; but she prayed for safety, gathered the nettles and carried them back to the palace.

But not unnoticed. One person had seen and followed her; the archbishop. So his suspicions were true! The new Queen *was* a witch.

In the church, after the service, he told all this to the King. The carved saints shook their heads as if to say – "It is not so! Elisa is innocent!" But the archbishop chose to take this differently; the saints were bearing witness against her. They were shaking their heads at her sins.

Two heavy tears rolled down the King's face, and he went home with a troubled heart. He pretended to sleep at night, but no sleep came. Now, day by day, he grew more wretched. This troubled Elisa sorely, and added to her grief about her brothers. Her tears ran down her royal velvet and purple and lay there like diamonds; but people saw only her beauty and her rich attire and wished that *they* were Queen.

Still, her task was nearly done, for only a single shirt remained to be made. The trouble was that again she had no more flax, not a single nettle.

Once more she would have to go back to the churchyard. She thought fearfully of the lonely midnight journey; but then she thought of her brothers.

She went — and the King and the archbishop followed her. They saw her disappear through the iron gates of the churchyard; they saw the frightful lamias on the graves. The King turned away in grief, for he thought that she had come to seek the company of these monsters — his own Elisa, his Queen.

"The people shall judge her!" he said. And this the people did. They proclaimed her guilty, and ordered her to be burnt at the stake.

She was taken from the splendor of the palace and thrust into a dungeon, damp and dark. Instead of silken sheets and velvet pillows, the nettles and nettle-work cloth from her room had been tossed in. But she could have asked for no better gift. While boys outside sang jeering songs — "The witch! The witch!" — she began to work on the last of the shirts.

The archbishop had arranged to spend the final hours in prayer with her; but when he came, Elisa shook her head and pointed to the door. Her work must be finished that night. The archbishop went away, muttering angry words.

Poor Elisa! If only she could speak. Little mice ran over the floor; they dragged the nettles towards her, doing all that they could to help. A thrush sang all night through at the bars to give her hope.

At first light, an hour before sunrise, the eleven brothers, in human form, stood at the castle gate and demanded to see the King. Impossible! was the answer. The King was asleep and could not be disturbed. They begged and pleaded; they threatened; the guard came down to see what the noise was about. At last it brought down the King himself.

At that very moment the sun rose. Where were the eleven young men? Nowhere. But over the palace flew eleven wild swans.

From earliest daylight, crowds of people had jostled through the city gates; they all wanted to see the burning of the witch. There she was, in a cart dragged along by a forlorn old horse. She was wearing a smock made from coarse sacking; her lovely hair hung loose about her face; her cheeks were deathly pale, but her fingers never stopped working at the last of the green nettle shirts. The other ten lay at her feet. The crowds mocked and yelled: "Look at the witch! See what she's up to! Still at her filthy witchcraft! Get it away from her! Tear it into a thousand pieces!"

They surged forward, and were just about to destroy her precious handiwork when down flew eleven great white swans. Beating their wings, they settled on the cart. The mob drew back in fear.

"It's a sign from heaven," some of them whispered. "She must be innocent."

The executioner seized her hand — but she quickly flung the eleven garments over the swans. In their place were eleven handsome princes. Only the youngest had a swan's wing instead of an arm, because Elisa had not had time to finish the last sleeve.

"Now I may speak," she said. "I am no witch. I am innocent."

The people hung their heads and kneeled before her.

"Yes, indeed she is innocent," said the eldest brother. And he began to tell their long, strange story. As he spoke, a fragrance as from millions of roses filled the air; every piece of wood in

the stake had taken root and put forth branches. There stood a mighty bush of the loveliest red roses. High at the summit was a single white flower, shining like a star. The King reached up and plucked it and laid it on Elisa's heart.

Then all the church bells rang of their own accord, and great flocks of birds flew overhead. And so began the journey back to the palace. A more joyful and more marvellous procession no King has ever yet seen.

The
Little Match Girl

HANS CHRISTIAN ANDERSEN ~ ILLUSTRATED
BY RACHEL ISADORA

IT WAS LATE on a bitterly cold New Year's Eve. The snow was
falling. A poor little girl was wandering in the dark cold streets; she
was bareheaded and barefoot.

She had of course had slippers on when she left home, but they were
not much good, for they were so huge. They had last been worn by her
mother, and they fell off the poor little girl's feet when she was running
across the street to avoid two carriages that were rolling rapidly by. One
of the shoes could not be found at all, and the other was picked up by a
boy who ran off with it, saying that it would do for a cradle when he had
children of his own.

So the poor little girl had to walk on with her little bare feet, which were red and blue with the cold. She carried a quantity of matches in her old apron, and held a packet of them in her hand. Nobody had bought any from her during all the long day, and nobody had even given her a copper. The poor little creature was hungry and perishing with cold, and she looked the picture of misery.

The snowflakes fell on her long yellow hair, which curled so prettily round her face, but she paid no attention to that. Lights were shining from every window, and there was a most delicious odor of roast goose in the streets, for it was New Year's Eve. She could not forget that!

She found a corner where one house projected a little beyond the next one, and here she crouched, drawing up her feet under her, but she was colder than ever. She did not dare to go home, for she had not sold any matches and had not earned a single penny. Her father would beat her, and besides it was as cold at home as it was here. They had only the roof over them, and the wind whistled through it although they stuffed up the biggest cracks with rags and straw.

Her little hands were almost stiff with cold. Oh, one little match would do some good! If she only dared, she would pull one out of the packet and strike it on the wall to warm her fingers. She pulled out one. *R-r-sh-sh!* How it sputtered and blazed! It burnt with a bright clear flame, just like a little candle, when she held her hand round it.

Now the light seemed very strange to her! The little girl fancied that she was sitting in front of a big stove with polished brass feet and handles. There was a splendid fire blazing in it and warming her so beautifully, but — what happened?

Just as she was stretching out her feet to warm them, the flame went out, the stove vanished — and she was left sitting with the end of the burnt match in her hand.

She struck a new one. It burnt, it blazed up, and where the light fell upon the wall, it became transparent like gauze, and she could see right through it into the room. The table was spread with a snowy cloth and pretty china. A roast goose stuffed with apples and prunes was steaming on it. And what was even better, the goose hopped from the dish with the carving knife sticking in his back and waddled across the floor. It came right up to the poor child, and then — the match went out, and there was nothing to be seen but the thick black wall.

She lit another match. This time she was sitting under a lovely Christmas tree. It was much bigger and more beautifully decorated than the one she had seen when she peeped through the glass doors at the rich

merchant's house this very Christmas. Thousands of lighted candles gleamed under its branches. And many colored pictures, such as she had seen in the shop windows, looked down at her.

The little girl stretched out both her hands towards them — then out went the match. All the Christmas candles rose higher and higher, till she saw that they were only the twinkling stars. One of them fell and made a bright streak across the sky.

Someone is dying, thought the little girl, for her old grandmother, the only person who had ever been kind to her, used to say, "When a star falls, a soul is going up to God."

Now she struck another match against the wall, and this time it was her grandmother who appeared in the circle of flame. She saw her quite clearly and distinctly, looking so gentle and happy.

"Grandmother!" cried the little creature. "Oh, do take me with you. I know you will vanish when the match goes out. You will vanish like the warm stove, the delicious goose, and the beautiful Christmas tree!"

She hastily struck a whole bunch of matches, because she did so long to

keep her grandmother with her. The light of the matches made it as bright as day. Grandmother had never before looked so big or so beautiful. She lifted the little girl up in her arms, and they soared in a halo of light and joy, far, far above the earth, where there was no more cold, no hunger, and no pain – for they were with God.

In the cold morning light the poor little girl sat there, in the corner between the houses, with rosy cheeks and a smile on her face – dead. Frozen to death on the last night of the old year. New Year's Day broke on the little body still sitting with the ends of the burnt-out matches in her hand.

"She must have tried to warm herself," they said. Nobody knew what beautiful visions she had seen, nor in what a halo she had entered with her grandmother upon the glories of the New Year.

The Steadfast Tin Soldier

HANS CHRISTIAN ANDERSEN ~ TRANSLATED BY ERIK HAUGAARD
AND ILLUSTRATED BY BERT KITCHEN

ONCE THERE WERE five and twenty tin soldiers. They were all brothers because they had been made from the same old tin spoon. With their rifles sticking up over their shoulders, they stood at attention, looking straight ahead, in their handsome red and blue uniforms.

"Tin soldiers!" were the first words they heard in this world; and they had been shouted happily by a little boy who was clapping his hands because he had received them as a birthday gift. He took them immediately out of the box they had come in and set them on the table. They were all exactly alike except one, who was different from the others because he was missing a leg. He had been the last one to be cast and there had not been enough tin. But he stood as firm and steadfast on his one leg as the others did on their two. He is the hero of our story.

Of all the many toys on the table, the one you noticed first was a pasteboard castle. It was a little replica of a real castle, and through its windows you could see right into its handsomely painted halls. In front of the castle was a little lake surrounded by trees; in it swans swam and looked at their own reflections because the lake was a glass mirror. It was all very lovely; but the most charming part of the castle was its mistress.

She was a little paper doll and she was standing in the entrance dressed like a ballerina. She had a skirt of white muslin and a blue ribbon draped over her shoulder, which was fastened with a spangle that was almost as large as her face. The little lady had her arms stretched out, as if she were going to embrace someone. She stood on one leg, and at that on her toes, for she was a ballet dancer; the other, she held up behind her, in such a way that it disappeared under her skirt; and therefore the soldier thought that she was one-legged like himself.

"She would be a perfect wife for me," he thought. "But I am afraid she is above me. She has a castle and I have only a box that I must share with twenty-four soldiers; that wouldn't do for her. Still, I would like to make her acquaintance." And the soldier lay down full length behind a snuffbox; from there he could look at the young lady, who was able to stand on the toes of only one leg without losing her balance.

Later in the evening, when it was the children's bedtime, all the other tin soldiers were put back in the box. When the house was quiet and everyone had gone to bed, the toys began to play. They played house, and hide-and-seek, and held a ball. The four and twenty tin soldiers rattled

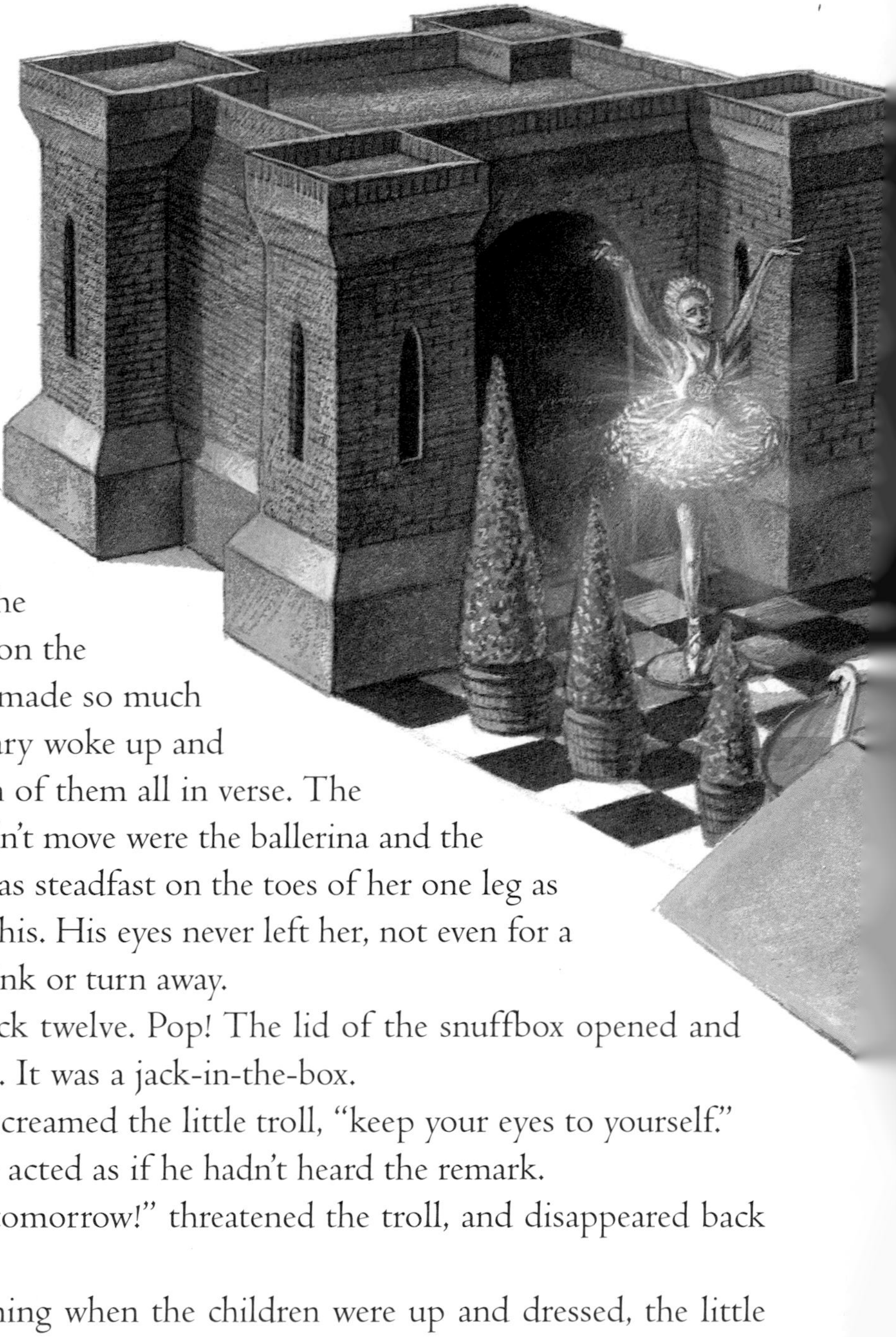

inside
their box;
they wanted
to play too, but
they couldn't get
the lid off. The
nutcracker turned
somersaults, and the
slate pencil wrote on the
blackboard. They made so much
noise that the canary woke up and
recited his opinion of them all in verse. The
only ones who didn't move were the ballerina and the
soldier. She stood as steadfast on the toes of her one leg as
the soldier did on his. His eyes never left her, not even for a
moment did he blink or turn away.

The clock struck twelve. Pop! The lid of the snuffbox opened and
out jumped a troll. It was a jack-in-the-box.

"Tin soldier," screamed the little troll, "keep your eyes to yourself."

The tin soldier acted as if he hadn't heard the remark.

"You wait till tomorrow!" threatened the troll, and disappeared back
into its box.

The next morning when the children were up and dressed, the little
boy put the one-legged soldier on the window sill. It's hard to tell
whether it was the troll or just the wind that caused the window to open
suddenly and the soldier to fall out of it. He dropped down three stories

to the street and his bayonet stuck in the earth between two cobblestones.

The boy and the maid came down to look for him and, though they almost stepped on him, they didn't see him. If only the tin soldier had shouted, "Here I am!" they would have found him; but he thought it improper to shout when in uniform.

It began to rain; first one drop fell and then another and soon it was pouring. When the shower was over two urchins came by. "Look," said one of them, "there is a tin soldier. He will do as a sailor."

The boys made a boat out of a newspaper, put the tin soldier on board, and let it sail in the gutter. Away it went, for it had rained so hard that the gutter was a raging torrent. The boys ran along on the pavement, clapping their hands. The boat dipped and turned in the waves. The tin soldier trembled and quaked inside himself; but outside, he stood as steadfast as ever, shouldering his gun and looking straight ahead.

Now the gutter was covered by a board. It was as dark as it had been inside the box, but there he had had four and twenty comrades. "I wonder how it will all end," thought the soldier. "I am sure it's all the troll's doing. If only the ballerina were here, then I wouldn't care if it were twice as dark as pitch."

A big water rat that lived in the gutter came up behind the boat and shouted, "Have you got a passport? Give me your passport!"

The tin soldier didn't answer but held more firmly on to his rifle. The current became stronger, and the boat gathered speed. The rat swam after him; it was so angry that it gnashed its teeth. "Stop him! Stop him!" the rat shouted to two pieces of straw and a little twig. "Stop him! He hasn't got a passport and he won't pay duty!"

The current ran swifter and swifter. The tin soldier could see light ahead; he was coming out of the tunnel. But at the same moment he heard a strange roaring sound. It was frightening enough to make the bravest man cringe. At the end of the tunnel the gutter emptied into one of the canals of the harbor. If you can imagine it, it would be the same as for a human being to be thrown down a great waterfall into the sea.

There was no hope of stopping the boat. The poor tin soldier stood as steady as ever, he did not flinch. The boat spun round four times and became filled to the brim with water. It was doomed, the paper began to fall apart; the tin soldier was standing in water up to his neck. He thought of the ballerina, whom he would never see again, and two lines from a poem ran through his mind.

"Fare thee well, my warrior bold,
Death comes so swift and cold."

The paper fell apart and the tin soldier would have sunk down into the mud at the bottom of the canal had not a greedy fish swallowed him just at that moment.

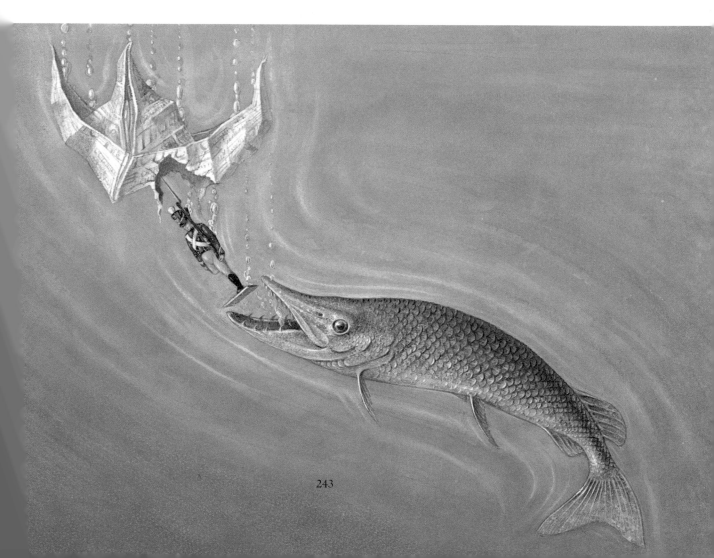

243

Here it was even darker than it had been in the sewer; the fish's stomach was terribly narrow, but the soldier lay there as steadfast as he had stood in the boat, without letting go of his rifle.

The fish darted and dashed in the wildest manner; then suddenly it was still. A while later, a ray of light appeared and someone said, "Why, there is a tin soldier." The fish had been caught, taken to the market, and sold. The kitchen maid had found the soldier when she opened the fish up with a big knife, in order to clean it. With her thumb and her index

finger she picked the tin soldier up by the waist and carried him into the living room, so that everyone could admire the strange traveller who had journeyed inside the belly of a fish. But the tin soldier was not proud of his adventures.

How strange the world is! He was back in the same room that he had left in the morning; and he had been put down on the table among the toys he knew. There stood the cardboard castle and the little ballerina. She was still standing on one leg, the other she had lifted high into the air. She was as steadfast as he was. It touched the soldier's heart and he almost cried tin tears — and would have, had it not been so undignified. He looked at her and she at him, but never a word passed between them.

Suddenly one of the little boys grabbed the soldier, opened the stove, and threw him in. The child couldn't explain why he had done it; there's no question but that the jack-in-the-box had had something to do with it.

The tin soldier stood illuminated by the flames that leaped around him. He did not know whether the great heat he felt was caused by his love or the fire. The colors of his uniform had disappeared, and who could tell whether it was from sorrow or his trip through the water? He looked at the ballerina, and she looked at him. He could feel that he was melting; but he held on as steadfastly as ever to his gun and kept his gaze on the little ballerina in front of the castle.

The door of the room was opened, a breeze caught the little dancer and like a sylph she flew right into the stove. She flared up and was gone. The soldier melted. The next day when the maid emptied the stove, she found a little tin heart, which was all that was left of him. Among the ashes lay the metal spangle from the ballerina's dress; it had been burned as black as coal.

Beauty and the Beast

JEANNE-MARIE LEPRINCE DE BEAUMONT ~ RETOLD BY ELIZABETH
RUDD AND ILLUSTRATED BY RACHEL ISADORA

L ONG AGO IN A FARAWAY LAND lived a rich merchant and his
family: three daughters and three sons. Their mother had died when
they were young, leaving them to the care of their father who spoiled
them. The family lived in a beautiful palace: their every wish and whim
attended to by a multitude of servants. This was not all for the good.
The merchant's sons thought of nothing but hunting and sport, whilst
his eldest daughters became snobbish and arrogant. Only his youngest
daughter remained unaffected by the luxury which surrounded them.
And, as the years passed, she was known to everyone as Beauty because,
quite simply, that is what she was. She loved the animals, the rivers and
lakes, the flowers and the forests of her father's vast estate and was never
happier than when enjoying the simple pleasures of the countryside. She
always had a kindly word for the poor and unfortunate, quite unlike her
older sisters who despised poverty. She was, of course, her father's favorite.

Then disaster struck. A messenger arrived at the palace and told of a
violent storm off the coast of Africa. The merchant's fleet of ships, fully
laden with precious cargo, was battered against a cruel reef by
mountainous seas. Not one ship nor one brave sailor survived. The
merchant had risked his entire fortune on this expedition: he was ruined.
The estate, its contents, servants and horses; all must go. They would
have just enough money to buy a country cottage and a few acres of land
from which they might scratch a living.

His sons took the harsh news bravely and promised to work in the fields. But his eldest daughters were furious. They cursed their father for his folly and declared that to live in a modest cottage would kill them. Beauty was least troubled by the loss of her comforts but sad to see her father's misery.

Taking with them one horse and a faithful old servant the family settled down to a peasant way of life. Beauty's father and brothers worked on the land, whilst she did all the housework and tended the vegetable garden. Her sisters spent all their time lamenting their losses.

Many months had passed, when news came that one of the merchant's ships had weathered the storm and was making for port. Hearing these tidings, the merchant saddled his horse and set off to meet the ship. His two elder daughters made a list of the presents they would expect upon his return. Beauty, though, asked for nothing but some flowers which she loved but could no longer spare time to grow. So the merchant set off on a journey which he hoped would restore his fortunes.

Alas, he was due for a bitter disappointment. True, his ship and

precious cargo had arrived intact, but so had his creditors with writs of law claiming everything. Wearily he turned for home, not a single penny better off. Tired and hungry, not knowing how to break the miserable news to his family, he let his horse stray and was soon lost in the depths of the forest. The horse halted in a clearing by a high wall in which stood an open door. It seemed as if he were expected.

He led his mount through the doorway and into the magnificent courtyard of a fine castle. To one side were stables where a warm stall with water and oats awaited his tired horse. But not a soul was in attendance. Timidly, he entered the castle by a side entrance.

Burning torches lit his way to a dining hall where, before a blazing log fire, a table was laid for dinner. He called aloud, but no sound could be heard throughout the vast dwelling.

He warmed himself at the fire for a few minutes and, when he turned back to the table, saw to his astonishment that wine was served and a splendid dinner laid out, ready to be eaten. He waited for someone to appear, but no one did. Famished, he sat down and ate heartily. Then, as if sensing his exhaustion, torches lit his way up a grand staircase to a comfortable bedroom where he laid himself down to sleep.

The following morning, refreshed and anxious to thank his host, he hurried downstairs, but there was no sign of life. He found breakfast waiting and there in the courtyard, groomed and fresh, his horse champed impatiently. Lost in wonder he took the bridle and led the steed out the way he had entered. Then, turning for a final look at the mysterious castle, he noticed white roses trailing over the wall and remembered Beauty's request. He gathered a small bunch, glad that he could at least please one of his daughters.

As he did so, he heard a terrible roar and there, before him, loomed a hideous beast. "Villain," screamed the beast. "You have enjoyed my hospitality but that is not enough. You must steal my property." The merchant, frightened for his life, sank to his knees.

"Oh no, sir. I am deeply grateful," he cried. "But I could see no one to thank. I meant no harm."

"You presume too much and will answer for it with your life," roared the beast.

"Alas," sobbed the merchant, "I shall never see Beauty again."

"Beauty," growled the beast. "Who is this Beauty? Be quick and explain."

So the merchant told of his misfortune, his journey and of his youngest daughter whose simple request had led him to trespass. The beast's anger subsided. "I shall spare your life on the condition that your daughter returns here to take your place."

The merchant knew he could never leave his beloved daughter in the care of such a monster, but to pretend to agree would at least allow him to see her again.

"You will be provided with money to pay for your daughter's journey here. But do not attempt to deceive me. Now be gone!" said the beast. And with a bound he disappeared.

Unseen hands had placed a saddlebag across the horse's back; in the left-hand pocket of the bag were gold coins and in the right precious jewels. His horse quickly found its way through the forest and within two hours he was home. The elder daughters were all agog when they saw the wealth contained in the saddlebag. Beauty was delighted to see her father safe home, but she could see that he was troubled. For a while the merchant could not bring himself to spoil his children's high spirits; then he could keep the truth from them no longer.

When they heard the beast's demand for Beauty his sons were angry. "We shall find this beast and kill it," they declared.

"Impossible," said their father, "the beast has many strange powers. You are no match for it. I must return and meet my fate."

Then Beauty spoke. "To go back on your word might anger the beast further and bring disaster on us all. I shall go to the beast as you promised and perhaps I may reason with him and calm his fury."

The despairing merchant and his sons tried in vain to dissuade Beauty from her brave decision. Her sisters pretended to be concerned, moaning and crying false tears. However, they only cared for the jewels and were jealous of the attention given to their younger sister.

In the morning Beauty said goodbye to her weeping father, her sad brothers and her deceitful sisters. As if guided by magic the horse carried her swiftly to the castle of the beast.

Fearful, but determined to be brave, Beauty entered the castle. It was deserted. At the far end of a magnificent hall was a staircase leading to a door; trembling, she approached. The door opened of its own accord and beyond was the most marvellous suite of rooms she had ever seen: a sitting room with frames for needlework and embroidery awaiting a skilled hand; paints and canvas to delight any artist; a music room with gold instruments and an ivory piano; a dressing room, its wardrobe crammed with beautiful gowns; and a bedroom with a balcony overlooking a fine garden.

She explored every inch of the apartment finding new delights as she went. At evening time, a fire was lit in her sitting room and a table set. A delicious supper was served by invisible servants. When the meal was finished, Beauty heard strange scuffling noises followed by a loud knock. Her heart leapt to her mouth, but she summoned her courage and in a clear, calm voice called, "Please enter."

The beast shuffled in. Beauty was shocked at his horrifying appearance, but tried not to show it.

"Was supper to your liking?" asked the beast in a gruff voice.

"It was the most delicious I have ever eaten," replied Beauty, truthfully.

Although it was difficult to detect any expression on the beast's face, he seemed pleased. Beauty was greatly relieved. "He surely cannot intend to harm me," she thought.

"May I sit and talk with you for a while?" asked the beast.

"Of course," replied Beauty, beginning to master her fear. They talked for a while about things of no great importance, then the beast rose and wished her a good night.

Beauty climbed into her huge silken bed and fell soundly asleep. And in her dreams a kindly lady appeared and told her to have no fears, for one day her good nature should be richly rewarded.

So the time passed pleasantly enough for Beauty in the castle of the beast. Every evening after dinner he would sit with her and talk, and as Beauty saw no one during the day she looked forward to his visits. Then one night, whilst they were sitting together, he asked, "Beauty, will you marry me?"

"Beast," said Beauty, "I will not deny that I have grown fond of you, but I could not marry you."

The beast turned away from her, his shoulders hunched. Beauty felt that he was terribly sad. So life at the castle carried on. Every evening the beast would enquire if all was to her satisfaction; and indeed everything was perfect, so Beauty could hardly complain. She did miss her father, though, and asked the beast for news of him. He said that when she was alone she must look into her dressing-table mirror and think hard of what she desired to see. This she did, and she saw her family plainly in the glass. Her father was well, although miserable; her brothers had joined the army; her sisters, with the help of the dowries provided by the beast's wealth, had married.

Thereafter Beauty was more content. Her days were filled with wonderful games, amusements and concerts; all provided by unseen attendants. Each day she grew ever more fond of the beast, no longer paying any heed to his ugliness. They talked and even laughed the night away most merrily. However, always their meetings ended the same way: the beast would confess that he loved her and ask her to marry him. Beauty would sadly decline, and the beast would say good night.

One day, whilst viewing her magic mirror for news of her family, she saw that her father was pining for her. She resolved to speak to the beast.

"Dear Beast," she implored, "I am terribly worried about my father. Would you not in your kindness let me return home for just a week?"

"Beauty, I cannot refuse you anything, but I fear this request," said the beast. "I dread that once you are home you will never return and I shall die of grief. However, it shall be as you wish. Take this ring and wear it when you go to bed tonight. Tomorrow you will find yourself back at your father's home. But after seven days you must return to me, Beauty. I cannot live without you. Do not break your promise."

Beauty retired to bed happy that night. When she woke the following morning it was as the beast had promised; she was in her father's cottage. He was overjoyed to see her. Once again, the beast had sent her with magnificent gifts, a trunk full of fine clothes and more gold than she could spend. Her sisters hurried to greet her along with their new husbands. They feigned pleasure at seeing her again; but were clearly as resentful as ever.

Her sisters' marriages were unhappy. One had married a young man so handsome that his only concern was for himself; the other a young man so clever that he spent all his time teasing his wife for her lack of wit.

When the two sisters saw Beauty's wealth and finery and heard that she lived in a castle, her every want attended to, they wept bitter tears of envy. They determined to do Beauty some mischief.

When it was time for her to keep her promise to return, her sisters begged her to stay longer. It was their hope to bring the beast's wrath down on her, so that she would lose everything, even her life. And so Beauty stayed on with her father and sisters. Then, on the ninth night of her visit, Beauty had such a sad dream that she awoke in tears. She dreamt of the beast's garden; there the beast lay, weak, almost dead. At once she realized how much she missed him and, indeed, how much she loved him. Taking from her finger the ring he had given her, she placed it on her bedside table and dearly wished to be by his side.

Instantly she was back in the castle. She ran through the great hall, calling desperately. Then out to the garden she ran, and down to the stream by which he lay, motionless. She took some water from the stream and gently bathed his head.

"Beauty," murmured the beast, "you broke your promise. I have missed you so badly, and now I am close to death."

"Oh, Beast," sobbed Beauty, "you must not die. Whilst absent from you I realized I love you dearly and would gladly marry you." Beauty's tears fell on the poor beast as she cradled his head in her arms. And as they fell, the most wonderful change occurred. There, in her arms instead of the beast, was the most handsome prince Beauty had ever seen.

"But what has become of Beast?" cried the startled Beauty.

"I am that same beast," said the young prince. "Many years ago an evil witch cast a spell on me: that I should take the form of a hideous beast until a girl, of great charm and beauty, should consent to be my wife. Until you came, Beauty, no one would overlook my ugliness and love me for myself alone. You shall be my bride and later, my Queen. Never will you lose my love and gratitude."

Now the castle that had once been so silent was alive with music and gaiety. The gracious lady who had comforted Beauty in a dream now appeared and brought Beauty's family to share her happiness. This lady made known her intent to punish Beauty's ill-natured sisters, but Beauty pleaded for them and she relented.

And so Beauty journeyed to the kingdom of the prince, where they married and lived ever after in complete happiness.

The Red Shoes

HANS CHRISTIAN ANDERSEN ~ TRANSLATED BY
ERIK HAUGAARD AND ILLUSTRATED
BY QUENTIN BLAKE

ONCE THERE WAS A LITTLE GIRL who was delicate and lovely but very poor. In the summer she had to go barefoot and in the winter she had to wear wooden shoes that rubbed against her poor little ankles and made them red and sore.

In the same village there lived an old widow whose husband had been a shoemaker; and she was sewing a pair of shoes from scraps of red material. She did her very best, but the shoes looked a bit clumsy, though they were sewn with kindness. They were meant for the poor little girl, whose name was Karen.

Now on the very day that her mother was to be buried, Karen was given the red shoes. Though they weren't the proper color for mourning, she had no others, so she put them on. Raggedly dressed, bare-legged, with red shoes on her feet, she walked behind the pauper's coffin.

A big old-fashioned carriage drove by; in it sat an old lady. She noticed the little girl and felt so sorry for her that she went at once to the minister and spoke to him. "Let me have that little girl, and I shall be good to her and bring her up."

Karen thought it was because of her new red shoes that the old lady had taken a fancy to her. But the old lady declared that the shoes looked frightful and had them thrown into the stove and burned. Karen was dressed in nice clean clothes and taught to read and to sew. Everyone agreed that she was a very pretty child; but the mirror said, "You are more than pretty, you are beautiful."

It happened that the Queen was making a journey throughout the country, and she had her daughter, the little princess, with her. Everywhere people streamed to see them. When they arrived at a castle near Karen's village, the little girl followed the crowd out there. Looking out of one of the great windows of the castle was the little princess. So that people could see her, she was standing on a little stool. She had no crown on her head but she wore a very pretty white dress and the loveliest red shoes, made from morocco. They were certainly much prettier than the ones the old shoemaker's widow had made for Karen. But even they had been red shoes, and to Karen nothing else in the world was so desirable.

Karen became old enough to be confirmed. She was to have a new dress and new shoes for this solemn occasion. The old lady took her to

the finest shoemaker in the nearby town and he measured her little foot. Glass cabinets filled with the most elegant shoes and boots covered the walls of his shop. But the old lady's eyesight was so poor that she didn't get much out of looking at the display. Karen did; between two pairs of boots stood a pair of red shoes just like the ones the princess had worn.

Oh, how beautiful they were! The shoemaker said that they had been made for the daughter of a count but that they hadn't fitted her.

"I think they are patent leather," remarked the old lady. "They shine."

"Yes, they shine!" sighed Karen as she tried them on. They fitted the child and the old woman bought them. Had she known that they were red, she wouldn't have because it was not proper to wear red shoes when you were being confirmed. But her eyesight was failing – poor woman! – and she had not seen the color.

Everyone in the church looked at Karen's feet, as she walked towards the altar. On the walls of the church hung paintings of the former ministers and their wives who were buried there; they were portrayed wearing black with white ruffs round their necks. Karen felt that even they were staring at her red shoes.

When the old bishop laid his hands on her head and spoke of the solemn promise she was about to make — of her covenant with God to be a good Christian — her mind was not on his words. The ritual music was played on the organ; the old cantor sang, and the sweet voices of the children could be heard, but Karen was thinking of her red shoes.

By afternoon, everyone had told the old lady about the color of Karen's shoes. She was very angry and scolded the girl, telling her how improper it was to have worn red shoes in church, and that she must remember always to wear black ones, even if she had to put on an old pair.

Next Sunday Karen was to attend communion. She looked at her black shoes and she looked at her red shoes; then she looked at her red shoes once more and put them on.

The sun was shining, it was a beautiful day. The old lady and Karen took the path across the fields and their shoes got a bit dirty.

At the entrance to the church stood an old invalid soldier leaning on a crutch. He had a marvelously long beard that was red with touches of white in it. He bowed low towards the old lady and asked her permission to wipe the dust off her feet. Karen put her little foot forward too.

"What pretty little dancing shoes!" said the soldier and, tapping them on the soles, he added, "Remember to stay on her feet for the dance."

The old lady gave the soldier a penny, and she and Karen entered the church.

Again everyone looked at Karen's feet, even the people in the paintings on the walls. When she knelt in front of the altar and the golden cup was lifted to her lips, she thought only of the red shoes and saw them reflected in the wine. She did not join in the singing of the psalm and she forgot to say the Lord's Prayer.

The coachman had come with the carriage to drive them home from church. The old lady climbed in and Karen was about to follow her when the old soldier, who was standing nearby, remarked, "Look at those pretty dancing shoes."

His words made her take a few dancing steps. Once she had begun, her feet would not stop. It was as if the shoes had taken command of them. She danced round the corner of the church; her will was not her own.

The coachman jumped off the carriage and ran after her. When he finally caught up with her, he grabbed her and lifted her up from the ground, but her feet kept on dancing in the air, even after he managed to get her into the carriage. The poor old woman was kicked nastily while she and the coachman took Karen's shoes off her feet, so she could stop dancing.

When they got home, the red shoes were put away in a cupboard, but Karen could not help sneaking in to look at them.

The old lady was very ill. The doctors had come and said that she would not live much longer. She needed careful nursing and constant care, and who else but Karen ought to give it to her? In the town there was to be a great ball and Karen had been invited to go. She looked at the old lady, who was going to die anyway, and then she glanced at her red shoes. To glance was no sin. Then she put them on; that too did no great harm. But she went to the ball!

She danced! But when she wanted to dance to the left, the shoes danced to the right; and when she wanted to dance up the ballroom floor, the shoes danced right down the stairs and out into the street. Dance she did, out through the city gates and into the dark forest.

Something shone through the trees. She thought it was the moon because it had a face. But it was not; it was the old soldier with the red beard. He nodded to her and exclaimed, "Look what beautiful dancing shoes!"

Terrified, she tried to pull off her shoes. She tore her stockings but the shoes stayed on. They had grown fast to her feet. Dance she did! And dance she must! Over the fields and meadows, in the rain and sunshine, by night and by day. But it was more horrible and frightening at night when the world was dark.

"Now I have suffered enough because of those red shoes," thought Karen. "I shall go to church now and be among other people."

But when she walked up to the door of the church, the red shoes danced in front of her, and in horror she fled.

All during that week she felt sad and cried many a bitter tear. When Sunday came she thought, "Now I have suffered and struggled long enough. I am just as good as many of those who are sitting and praying in church right now, and who dare to throw their heads back with pride." This reasoning gave her courage, but she came no farther than the gate of the churchyard. There were the shoes dancing in front of her. In terror she fled, but this time she really repented in the depth of her heart.

She went to the minister's house and begged to be given work. She said that she did not care about wages but only wanted a roof over her head and enough to eat. The minister's wife hired the poor cripple because she felt sorry for her. Karen was grateful that she had been given a place to live and she worked hard. In the evening when the minister read from the Bible, she sat and listened thoughtfully. The children were fond of her and she played with them, but when they talked of finery and being beautiful like a princess, she would sadly shake her head.

When Sunday came, everyone in the household got ready for church, and they asked her to go with them. Poor Karen's eyes filled with tears. She sighed and glanced towards her crutches.

When the others had gone, she went into her little room that was so small that a bed and a chair were all it could hold. She sat down and began to read from her psalmbook. The wind carried the music from the church organ down to her, and she lifted her tear-stained face and whispered, "Oh, God, help me!"

Suddenly the sunlight seemed doubly bright and an angel of God stood before her. He was the same angel who with his sword had barred her entrance to the church, but now he held a rose branch covered with flowers. With this he touched the low ceiling of the room and it rose high into the air and, where he had touched it, a golden star shone. He touched the walls and they widened.

Karen saw the organ. She saw the old paintings of the ministers and their wives; and there were the congregation holding their psalmbooks in front of them and singing. The church had come to the poor girl in her little narrow chamber; or maybe she had come to the church. Now she sat among the others, and when they finished singing the psalm they looked up and saw her.

Someone whispered to her: "It is good that you came, Karen."

"This is His mercy," she replied.

The great organ played and the voices of the children in the choir mingled sweetly with it. The clear, warm sunshine streamed through the window. The sunshine filled Karen's heart till it so swelled with peace and happiness that it broke. Her soul flew on a sunbeam up to God; and up there no one asked her about the red shoes.

The Little Mermaid

HANS CHRISTIAN ANDERSEN ~ RETOLD BY JOSEPHINE POOLE
AND ILLUSTRATED BY PETER WEEVERS

F AR OUT AT SEA there is a secret place where the water is so very
deep that it is always perfectly still, and as clear as crystal. If you
could find that place, and leaning over the side of your boat look down –
down – down – it would be like looking through a telescope, into the
strange and beautiful country of the Mer people.

Here, once upon a time, lived a King who had six daughters. His wife
died when the youngest was born, so his old mother lived with them in
the palace. She was a fearfully proud old mermaid, who wore a dozen
oysters pinned to her tail; but she was good-natured, and very fond of her
granddaughters. When they were tired of tidying their gardens, or

playing with the catfish and dogfish which swam about the rooms of the palace, they would gather round her and beg for stories of the old days when she was young and travelled far and wide. They particularly loved to hear about the *upper world* as she called it, with its curious plants and singing fish (the old lady meant birds), and the busy seaside towns, and the people living in them.

"Patience, patience!" the grandmother would say. "You have only to wait until you are fifteen, and you will gain the freedom of the sea, just as I did! Then you can discover all these wonders for yourselves."

"I shall be the first to see them!" cried the eldest, with a whisk of her tail.

"And I shall be the last," mourned Marmara, the youngest. She often thought about the upper world, for in her garden there was a statue that had been brought to her from a shipwreck; it was a boy made of white marble, the most beautiful person she had ever seen. She was thrilled by the idea of a world where everyone looked like that.

And at last her turn came, on her fifteenth birthday. How beautiful she was, with pearls threading her hair, and a necklace of pink and white coral!

"I declare you are even prettier than your sisters!" said the grandmother. "Well, you are about to attain your heart's desire — I hope it won't be a disappointment!"

The six mermaids linked arms and floated slowly upwards, singing together. Only Marmara could not sing — she was too excited. Her face was turned to the light which grew stronger and stronger as they neared the surface. When her sisters kissed her and swam away, she forgot to say goodbye, she was so astonished by the water which danced and glittered in the sunshine as if it was alive. She took her first breaths of air, and was filled with a sparkling energy she had never felt before. She began swimming, tirelessly swimming, sometimes leaping over the little waves for joy — until the sun was low over the sea, until it seemed to burst on the horizon, and stain the water and the sky with blood.

In the distance a ship was moving slowly under one huge sail that barely swelled in the breeze. As Marmara came closer, she noticed strings of flags in the rigging. Lamps were being lit, and a band started to play. She swam right up to the hull. Anyone could then have seen her pale face at the porthole, but the people inside were laughing and talking as they helped themselves to food and wine. They were not nearly as beautiful as she expected, except for one — and everyone treated him respectfully, because he was a prince. Today was his sixteenth birthday.

The mermaid rocked gently on the waves, gazing at the beautiful boy whose birthday was the same day as her own. What would he do if she tapped on the porthole — if she sang to him when he came out on deck? Now they were dancing. How clumsy they looked! She longed for him to come out, so that she could show him the Mer way of dancing, as light as spray upon the sea!

It was quite dark now, and the weather was changing. The wind was ruffling the flags, making the lamps flare. The huge sail suddenly filled and the ship moved faster. The captain came out and ordered the sails to be reefed. The ship shuddered as the waves bumped her.

Marmara's white arms and silvery hair gleamed like moonbeams in the stormy water. She laughed as the see-saw waves tossed her up — until she looked again through the porthole. The prince had gone. His birthday feast was in ruins, and the remaining guests huddled together with very white faces.

The ship began to groan like a tormented beast every time a big wave struck. While Marmara was wondering what this could mean, a freak wind snapped the mast in two, and the reefed sails crashed down. The captain struggled to cut them loose, but it was useless. The ship staggered, lifted high on one last wave — and turned over.

Now, Marmara's only thought was to rescue the prince, and at last she

found him, drifting like a corpse with his eyes closed, at the mercy of the raging sea. She believed he was dead, but still she took him in her arms and swam with him all night. At dawn she saw land, and she had just enough strength to reach a cove where there was a cottage. She kissed his cold lips, and pushed him up on the sand. Then, with an aching heart, she swam out into the bay, but she did not go far, she meant to watch over his body until it was discovered.

The prince was not dead — only chilled to the bone. As the sun warmed him, it brought him back to life. The mermaid saw him move. She saw a beautiful child find him on the beach, and run for help. Her grief was turned to joy; yet she was a little sad, because she had saved him, but he would never know it.

When she returned to her father's palace, her grandmother was cross because she had lost her necklace; it must have been torn off during the storm. Her sisters were curious to hear of her adventures, but she had nothing to say. She could think of nothing but the prince, and as luck would have it she soon had news of him. A friend came to visit, and talked about the shipwreck, and how it was a miracle the prince had not been drowned. "He is quite beautiful, for an earth person," she added. "I know, for I have seen him in his palace on the edge of the sea."

So Marmara found out where he lived, and told herself that if she saw him just once more, safe and well, that would be enough. She arrived at nightfall; lights sparkled in every room in his palace, torches blazed on the steps that led up to it from the sea. She wished for him to come out, and so he did, almost at once — as if her longing put the thought into his mind.

She meant to sing to him, her own song about the shipwreck, and how she had saved his life. But the words died in her throat. She could only gaze at him and love him from a distance — how could she ever approach him? For the first time she hated her shimmering tail, because on land it would turn her into a clumsy creature.

It was not enough to see him just once more. She went constantly to his palace, and she imagined that he knew she was there, for he would walk alone along the shore, or stare out over the balcony, as if he was looking for someone. But she spent so much time away from home that her grandmother became suspicious.

"I suppose you think yourself in love," she said snappishly, when the princess had timidly answered her questions. "You should have left him to drown, death is nothing to earth people, they are not like us who die and turn to foam. They believe they have immortal souls which live for ever in heaven in perfect happiness."

"What is heaven? I wish I had an immortal soul. Oh, Grandmother!" Marmara cried piteously. "Is there no way of changing myself into an earth person?"

"Certainly not! I never heard of such a thing!" But still the old lady was glad of an opportunity to air her knowledge about the upper world. She went on, "There is only one way that you can acquire a soul. If your prince loved you so much that he carried you to church, and the priest joined you to him in holy marriage — why then the two of you would become one, and naturally you would share his soul."

"But couldn't that happen?" faltered Marmara.

"Don't be ridiculous! Whoever heard of a prince marrying a *mermaid*? Do you think he wants to share his throne with a *fish tail*? No, it would be quite impossible, and it is just as well, for believe me, no good would come of it."

The old Queen meant to deter her granddaughter, but her words had the opposite effect. The princess was now convinced that if she could only get rid of her tail, she would find eternal happiness: first with her prince, and after death in that place called heaven. She knew that only a powerful charm could change her shape, and she was afraid. But she loved more than she feared, and she made up her mind to visit the one person who might be able to help her.

This was a horrible old witch, who was very smelly and disgusting. She had a lap full of eels which she was feeding with live shrimps.

"Ha! I know what *you* want!" she cried as soon as she saw Marmara. "You want me to turn your tail into legs!" And her horrid red eyes glowed with glee. "Well, if I do, you'll never be able to turn back into a mermaid. And there's another thing. You'll be admired — you'll be the loveliest, most graceful maiden people have ever seen! But every step you take, my dear, will hurt as if you were treading on the blades of knives. What about that?"

Marmara thought of the prince. She remembered his immortal soul, which she might share. "I don't care," she said.

"All right! Now, what happens if your prince marries somebody else?" The mermaid was silent. "I'll tell you what. The morning after he marries another, at sunrise, your little heart will break, my dear! It will break for grief, and you will dissolve like foam on the sea. Well? Am I to work the charm, or not?"

"Yes," said the princess. But she was trembling all over.

The witch emptied the eels out of her lap and stood up. "How are you going to pay?" she demanded.

"I can give you pearls — "

"Pearls! No, thanks. I do fancy your beautiful voice though. I'll take that. Is it a bargain?"

"But how will the prince fall in love with me, if I can't speak?"

"It won't make any difference! Believe me, when he sees you dance — "

So the princess was persuaded to give up her voice. Then the witch boiled a brew, and stabbed herself so that her black blood dripped into the cauldron. And she boiled and boiled it until it was transformed into a thimbleful of clear, sparkling liquid.

"Here you are," she said, pouring it into a cockleshell. "Now you must pay your debts, like a true princess." And quick as a flash, she cut out Marmara's tongue.

Marmara wanted to see her family for the last time. She looked wistfully at them through the window of the palace; her father was singing, her grandmother had the catfish on her knee; her five sisters were dancing. She blew to each a farewell kiss; then, clutching the cockleshell, she left the Mer kingdom for ever.

She reached the prince's palace very early the next morning, and pulled herself up the steps. She swallowed the charm – and was transfixed with pain so frightful that she fainted. When she awoke, she knew at once that her tail had gone. She smiled, stretching her limbs, and opened her eyes. Her dear prince was bending over her. He helped her up – ah, then she felt the blades of knives! And she longed to speak, but could not.

The prince took her to his heart. She became his constant companion; because she couldn't speak, he told her his most secret

273

thoughts. One day he said, "My parents want me to marry, but the trouble is that I am already in love." Marmara's heart beat fast at these words, but he went on, "She saved my life when I was washed up on the beach. I shall never forget her face, though she was only a child. I would give anything to find her again."

"It was I who saved your life. It was I who swam all night with you in my arms," Marmara cried out to him in her heart. But not a word could she say. Oh, he loved her — she knew he loved her dearly — but as his devoted friend, not his bride!

Her sisters guessed where she had gone, and one evening, when she was on the balcony, they rose together out of the sea. They understood the terrible price she had paid for her human form. "What is the matter? Why are you stretching out your arms?" asked the prince. He saw nothing but the crests of the waves, heard nothing but the wind over the sea. So it was safe for them to visit her, and they came often.

Time passed, and the King and Queen heard of a girl who seemed ideal — not only beautiful and rich, but clever and kind as well. So the prince reluctantly agreed to meet her, and rode out at the head of a procession, with Marmara at his side. When they approached the mansion where the girl lived with her father, all the village children ran round them, throwing flowers, while she came out to greet them with her hand on her father's arm.

As soon as he saw her, the prince leapt from his horse. He had a feeling — he dared to hope — yes, it was true! and he ran the last steps to embrace the child, now grown into a beautiful woman, who he believed had once saved his life.

So Marmara had lost — not just human love, but her chance of eternal bliss. The prince was too happy to notice her sorrow. He planned to be married in a week; everyone was busy preparing for a splendid ceremony.

"And then I will die," said the voice of despair in Marmara's heart. "He will miss me at first, but he will soon forget. And I, who thought love and happiness would be mine for ever – I will no longer exist!"

She stared out to sea, to the cold grey sea where she belonged. Her sisters were her only comfort; she could not talk to them, but they found out all that had happened.

For the wedding Marmara wore a sea blue gown, with pearls round her neck and in her hair. Some said she looked even more beautiful than the bride, and she led the dancing, for nobody on earth could dance as well as she. Afterwards the fine company embarked on a ship painted scarlet and gold, with sails of brown silk. A light breeze wafted it from the shore, and rocked everyone to sleep. Only Marmara did not go to bed. This was the last night of her life, and she did not mean to waste it.

Towards dawn, when her anxious eyes already detected traces of pink in the east, her five sisters burst from the sea just below her. They had cut off their beautiful hair.

"We gave it to the witch," they cried. "We did it for you — " and one of them tossed up a knife which clattered down on the deck. "That is a charmed knife," said the eldest. "You must drive it into the heart of the prince, and then you will get back your tail, and leap down to us, and everything will be as it was before. But hurry – you must hurry! See, the sun is already touching the horizon! The prince must be killed before sunrise!"

Marmara picked up the knife. She knew where the prince and his bride were sleeping; she pushed past the embroidered curtain and crept in.

They lay side by side on the pillows. The prince was closest to her – how easy to plunge the knife into his heart! She looked down at his beloved face. She bent and kissed his lips, so gently that he did not stir. Then she slipped away. As she came up on deck, she saw the rising sun.

Her sisters had gone. She threw the knife into the sea, and stretched out her arms — and felt a tingling all through her, as if she was dissolving into champagne. And her sea blue gown dropped down on the deck, with her clusters of pearls.

Now she was floating, rising over the ship, while around her the sky was turning pink. Although she was invisible she could see and hear as well as ever, and she became aware of many voices. She understood what they said.

"Do not despair, dear little mermaid! All is not lost. The power of your love has turned you into a spirit of the air, and now you must fly with us, bringing hope to all the suffering unloved people in the world. And at last, when your work is done, you will take your place with the blessed in heaven."

The Snow Queen

HANS CHRISTIAN ANDERSEN ~ RETOLD BY NAOMI LEWIS
AND ILLUSTRATED BY ANGELA BARRETT

PART ONE
Which Tells of the Looking Glass and the Splinters

LISTEN NOW! We're going to begin our story. When we come to
the end of it we shall know more than we do now. There was once a
wicked imp, a demon, one of the very worst — he was the Devil himself.
One day, there he was, laughing his head off. Why? Because he had made
a magic mirror with a special power; everything good and beautiful that

was reflected in it shrivelled up almost to nothing, but everything evil and ugly seemed even larger and more hideous than it was. In this glass, the loveliest landscapes looked just like boiled spinach, and even the nicest people appeared quite horrible, or seemed to be standing on their heads, or to have no trunks to their bodies. As for their faces, they were so twisted and changed that no one could have recognized them; and, if anything holy and serious passed through someone's mind, a hideous sneering grin was shown in the glass. This was a huge joke.

All the students who attended his Demon School went round declaring that he'd achieved a miracle; now everyone could see what the world and its humans were really like. They took the mirror and ran round to the four corners of the earth, until there wasn't a place or person unharmed by the glass.

At last they fixed on a still more daring plan – to fly up to heaven, to make fun of the angels, and of God himself. The higher they flew with the mirror, the more it grimaced and twisted; they could scarcely hold on to it. Up and up they went, nearer and nearer to heaven's kingdom – until, disaster! The mirror shook so violently with its weird reflections that it sprang out of their hands and went crashing down to earth, where it burst into hundreds of millions, billions, trillions of tiny pieces. And that made matters even worse than before, for some of these pieces were hardly as big as a grain of sand. These flew here and there, all through the wide world; whoever got a speck in his eye saw everything good as bad or twisted – for every little splinter had the same power that the whole glass had had. Some people even caught a splinter in their hearts, and that was horrible, for their hearts became just like lumps of ice. Some of the pieces were so big that they were used as window panes – but it didn't do to look at your friends through them. Other pieces were made into spectacles – imagine! The demon laughed till he nearly split his sides.

And, as we tell this story, little splinters of magic glass are still flying about in the air. Listen! You shall hear what happened to some of them.

PART TWO
A Little Boy and a Little Girl

In a big city, where there are so many houses and people that there isn't room for everyone to have a garden, and so most people have to make do with flowers in pots, there once lived two poor children. But these two did have a garden a little larger than a flower pot. They were not brother and sister, but they were just as fond of each other as if they had been. Their parents were next-door neighbors; they lived in attics at the tops of next-door houses. Where the sloping roofs almost touched, a gutter ran along between; and across this, each house had a little window facing the other. You had only to step along the strip of roof to cross from window to window.

The parents each had a wooden box standing outside the window, and here they grew vegetables and herbs. They had little rose trees too, one in each box, and these grew gloriously. The pea plants trailed over the edges; the rose trees put out long branches, some twining around the windows, some bending over towards the opposite bush, making a kind of arch of leaves and flowers. The children would often sit on their little wooden stools under the roof of roses, and talk and play and spend many a happy hour.

In the winter, of course, there was no sitting out on the roof. The windows were often thick with frost, but the two children would warm up a coin on the stove, then press it on the frozen pane; this would make a splendid peep-hole. Behind each round hole was a bright and friendly eye, one at each window. These were the eyes of the little boy and the little girl; his name was Kay and hers was Gerda. In summer they could be together with a single jump, but in winter they had first to climb all the way down one lot of stairs, then up another – while outside the snow fell fast.

"Those are the white bees swarming," said the old grandmother.

"Have they a queen too?" asked the little boy, for he knew that real bees have.

"Yes, indeed," said the grandmother. "Wherever the flakes swarm most thickly, there she flies; she is the largest of them all. She never lies still on the ground, though, but soars up once again into the black cloud. On many a winter night she flies through the streets of the town and peers in at the windows, and then they freeze into the strangest patterns, like stars and flowers."

"Yes, I've seen that!" both children cried at once, knowing now that it must be true.

"Could the Snow Queen come in here?" asked the little girl.

"Just let her try!" said the boy. "I'll put her on the hot stove and then she'll melt."

But the grandmother smoothed his hair, and told them other stories.

In the evening, when little Kay was back at home and half undressed, he climbed on to the chair by the window and looked out through the little hole. A few snowflakes were drifting outside; then one of these, much larger than the rest, settled on the edge of the window-box outside. This snowflake grew and grew until it seemed to take the shape of a lady dressed in the finest white gauze, which was in fact made up of millions of tiny starlike flakes. She was so beautiful, wonderfully delicate and grand; but she was ice all through, dazzling, glittering ice — and yet she was alive. Her eyes blazed out like two bright stars, but there was no peace or rest in them. Now she nodded towards the window, and beckoned with her hand. The little boy was frightened and jumped down from the chair, and then he thought he saw a great bird go flying past.

The next day was clear and frosty; after that the thaw began; then it was spring. The sun shone; the first green shoots appeared; swallows built their nests; the windows were thrown open and the two children sat once more in their little roof garden.

The roses were so beautiful that summer, more than ever before. The little girl had learned a hymn which had a line about roses, and these made her think of her own. She sang the verse to the little boy, and he sang it too:

"In the vale the rose grows wild;
Children play all the day —
One of them is the Christ-child."

How lovely the summer was. The rose garden seemed as if it would never stop flowering.

Kay and Gerda were sitting looking at a picture book of birds and animals, and then — just as the clock in the great church tower began to strike five — Kay said, "Oh! Something pricked me in my heart! Oh! Now I've got something in my eye!"

The little girl put her arm round his neck, and he blinked his eyes. But no, there was nothing to be seen.

"I think it's gone," he said. But it hadn't. It was one of those tiny splinters from the demon's looking-glass — I'm sure you remember it. Poor Kay! He had got another piece right in his heart, which would soon be like a lump of ice. He didn't feel it, but it was there all right.

"Why are you crying?" he asked. "It makes you look horribly ugly. There's nothing the matter with me. Ugh!" he cried suddenly. "That rose has a worm in it. And look at that one — it's crooked. They're rotten, all of them. And the boxes, too." Then he kicked the boxes hard and tore off the two roses.

"Kay, what are you doing?" cried the little girl. And when he saw how frightened she was, he tore off a third rose, and ran in at his window, away from his little friend Gerda.

After that, when she brought out the picture book, he said that it was baby-stuff. When the grandmother told them stories, he would always find fault, and argue. He would even walk close behind her, put on spectacles, and mimic her way of talking. It was so well done that it made the people laugh. Soon he could mimic the ways of everyone in the street, especially if they were odd or unpleasant. People used to say, "Oh, he's clever, that boy!" But all this came from the splinters of glass in his eye and in his heart; they made him tease even little Gerda, who loved him more than anything in the world.

His games had become quite different now; they were so scientific and practical. One winter's day, as the snowflakes drifted down, he brought out a magnifying glass, then held out the corner of his blue jacket to catch some falling flakes.

"Now look through the glass, Gerda," he said. And she saw that every flake was very much larger, and looked like a splendid flower or a ten-pointed star. It was certainly a wonderful sight. "Look at that pattern — isn't it marvellous!" said Kay. "These are much more interesting than real flowers — and there isn't a single fault in them. They're perfect — if only they didn't melt."

A little later Kay came back wearing big gloves and carrying his sledge on his back. He shouted into Gerda's ear, "They're letting me go tobogganing in the town square where the others are playing!" And away he went.

Out in the square the boldest boys would often tie their sledges to farmers' carts, and so be pulled along for quite a ride. It was enormous fun. This time, while their games were in full swing, a very large sledge arrived; it was painted white all over, and in it sat a figure muffled up in a white fur cloak and wearing a white fur hat. This sledge drove twice round the square; but, moving quickly, Kay managed to fix his own sledge behind it, and a swift ride began. The big sledge went faster and faster, then turned off into the next street. The driver looked round and nodded to Kay in the friendliest fashion, just as if they had always known each other. Every time that Kay thought of unfastening his sledge, the driver would turn and nod to him again, so he kept still. On they drove, straight out of the city gates. And now the snow began to fall so thick and fast that the little boy couldn't even see his hand in front of him as they rushed along. At last he *did* manage to untie the rope but it was of no use; his little sledge still clung to the big one, and they sped along like the wind. He cried out at the top of his voice, but no one heard him; the snow fell, and the sledge raced on. From time to time it seemed to jump, as if they were going over dykes and hedges. Terror seized him; he tried to say the Lord's Prayer, but all he could remember was the multiplication table.

The snowflakes grew bigger and bigger, until at last they looked like great white birds. All at once they swerved to one side; the sledge came to a halt, and the driver stood up. The white fur cloak and cap were all of snow and the driver — ah, she was a lady, tall and slender, dazzlingly white! She was the Snow Queen herself.

"We've come far and fast," she said. "But you must be frozen. Creep under my bearskin cloak." She put him beside her in the sledge and wrapped the cloak around him; he felt as if he were sinking into a snowdrift. "Are you still cold?" she asked, and she kissed him on the forehead. Ah-h-h! Her kiss was colder than ice; it went straight to his heart, which was already halfway to being a lump of ice. He felt as if he were dying, but only for a moment. Then he felt perfectly well, and no longer noticed the cold.

"My sledge! Don't forget my sledge!" That was the first thought that came to him. So it was tied to one of the big white birds, which flew along with the little sledge at its back. The Snow Queen kissed Kay once again, and after that he had no memory of Gerda and the grandmother, nor of anyone at home.

"Now I must give you no more kisses," said the Snow Queen, "or you will be kissed to death."

Kay looked at her. She was so beautiful; he could not imagine a wiser, lovelier face. She no longer seemed to him to be made of ice, as she once had seemed when she came to the attic window and waved to him. Now in his eyes she was perfect, and he felt no fear. He told her that he could do mental arithmetic, and fractions too; that he knew the square miles of all the principal countries, and the number of inhabitants. As he

talked she smiled at him, until he began to think that what he knew was, after all, not quite so much. And he looked up into the vast expanse of the sky, as they rose up high, and she flew with him over the dark clouds, while the storm-wind whistled and raved, making him think of ballads of olden time. Over forest and lake they flew, over sea and land; beneath them screamed the icy blast; the wolves howled, the snow glittered; the black crows soared across the plains, cawing as they went. But high over all shone the great clear silver moon, and Kay gazed up at it all through the long, long winter night. During the day he slept at the Snow Queen's feet.

PART THREE
The Enchanted Flower Garden of the Old Woman
Who Understood Magic

But what of little Gerda when Kay did not return? Where could he be? No one knew; no one had any idea. The only thing that the boys could say was that they had seen him tie his little sledge to a big one, which drove out into the street and through the city gate. But who could tell what happened after that? There was great grief in the town; little Gerda wept many tears. Then people began to say that he must be dead, that he had fallen into the river that flowed past the city walls. Oh, what a long dark winter it was!

At last came the spring, and the first warm sunshine.

"Kay is dead and gone," said little Gerda.

"*I* don't believe it," said the sunshine.

"He is dead and gone," she said to the swallows.

"*I* don't believe it," declared each of the swallows. And at last little Gerda didn't believe it either.

"I will put on my new red shoes," she said one morning, "the ones Kay has never seen, and I'll go down and ask the river."

It was still very early when she kissed her sleeping grandmother, put on the red shoes, and walked all alone through the city gate and down to the river.

"Is it true that you have taken my little playmate?" she said. "I'll give you my red shoes if you'll let me have him back."

The waves, she thought, nodded back to her very strangely. So she took off her red shoes, the most precious thing she owned, and threw them into the water. But they fell close to the bank, and the little waves carried them straight back to her. It seemed just as if the river would not accept her dearest possession because it hadn't taken little Kay. But then Gerda felt that perhaps she hadn't thrown the shoes out far enough, so she climbed into a boat that lay among the rushes, and went to the further end of it, and threw the shoes again. But the boat had not been moored fast, and the movement made it float away from the shore. It began to glide away, gathering speed all the time.

At this little Gerda was very much frightened and began to cry, only nobody heard her except the sparrows, and they couldn't carry her ashore. But they flew along the bank, singing as if to comfort her, "Here we are! Here we are!" On sped the boat while little Gerda sat quite still in her stockinged feet. Her red shoes floated behind, but they couldn't catch the boat, which was now moving faster and faster.

The scene was pretty enough on both sides of the water; there were lovely flowers, old trees and grassy meadows with sheep and cows, but there wasn't a person in sight.

"Perhaps the river is carrying me to little Kay," thought Gerda, and her spirits began to rise. She stood up, and gazed for hour after hour at the beautiful green banks. At last she came to a cherry orchard, in which stood a little house with curious red and blue windows and a thatched roof; standing outside were two wooden soldiers, presenting arms whenever anyone passed. Gerda called out to them, thinking that they were alive, but of course they gave no answer. The river seemed to be driving the boat towards the bank, and Gerda called out even more pleadingly. Then, from the cottage, came an old, old woman, leaning on a crutch-shaped stick. She wore a large sun-hat, painted all over with many kinds of lovely flowers.

"You poor little child!" said the old woman. "How ever did you come to be on this river, so far out in the wide world?" And she stepped into the water, hooked the boat with her crooked stick, pulled it ashore, and lifted little Gerda down.

"Now come and tell me who you are," said she, "and how you managed to reach my house."

So Gerda told her everything, and the old woman shook her head, and murmured, "Hm, hm!" And when Gerda had finished her tale, and asked if she had seen little Kay, the woman said that he hadn't yet passed by, but he was sure to come; she was not to worry, but to have a taste of her cherries, and see her flowers, which were more wonderful than any picture book; every one of them had a story to tell. Then she took Gerda into the little house, and locked the door.

The windows were very high up, and the glass in them was red and yellow and blue. The daylight shone very strangely into the room with all these colors. But on the table were the most delicious cherries, and Gerda was told that she might eat as many as she liked. While she was eating, the old woman combed her hair with a golden comb, and her hair curled fair and shining round her little face that was just like a rose.

"I've often thought I would fancy a nice little girl around, just like you," said the old woman. "We shall get on very well together, you shall see." And she combed away at Gerda's hair, and as she combed, the little girl was forgetting more and more her playmate Kay. For the old woman could manage a bit of magic, though she was by no means a wicked witch. She used her magic only now and then for her own pleasure — and just now her pleasure was to keep little Gerda. To make sure of this, she went into the garden and pointed her stick at each of the lovely rose-bushes; at once, each bush sank down into the black earth, as if it had never been. For the old woman feared that if Gerda saw the roses she would think of her own in the roof-boxes, and remember little Kay, and run off to take up her journey.

This done, she took Gerda out into the flower garden. Ah, that garden — you can't imagine what magical beauty and fragrance she found there. All the flowers that you could ever bring to mind were growing together in full bloom at one time. It was better than all the picture books. Gerda jumped with joy and played there until the sun went down behind the tall cherry trees. Then she was given a lovely bed, its red silk pillows stuffed with violets, and here she slept.

When morning came she went out again to play among the flowers in the radiant sunshine, and so many days were spent. Before long she knew every separate flower, and yet, although there were so many, she felt that one was missing — only she could not think which. Then one day, as she was sitting indoors, her eyes turned to the painted flowers on the old woman's sun-hat; the loveliest of all was a rose. The old woman had quite forgotten this when she had made the real ones disappear into the ground. See what happens when you don't keep your wits about you!

"Oh!" cried Gerda. "Why have I never seen any roses in the garden?" And she ran in and out of the flower beds, searching and searching, but not a rose was to be found. At last she sat down and cried; but her warm tears fell just where a rose tree had sunk down. At once the tree sprang up, as full of fresh flowers as when it disappeared. Gerda put her arms round it, and kissed the roses, and thought about those in the roof-garden of her home — and then she remembered Kay.

"Oh, what a lot of time I have lost!" said the little girl. "I set out to find Kay. Do you know where he is?" she asked the roses. "Do you think he is dead and gone?"

"No, he is not dead," said the roses. "We have been in the earth where the dead are, but Kay was not there."

"Oh, thank you," said Gerda; then she went over to the other flowers, and looked into their cups, and asked, "Do you know where little Kay is?"

But the flowers stood in the sun, each one dreaming its own story. And Gerda listened to all the tales and dreams, but of Kay there was never a word.

What did the convolvulus say?

"High above, overlooking the narrow mountain road, stands an ancient castle. Evergreen creepers grow thickly over the old red walls; leaf by leaf they twine round the balcony where a fair young girl leans over the balustrade, gazing down at the path below. No rose on its branch is fresher and lovelier; no apple blossom that floats from the tree is more delicate. Listen — her silk dress rustles as she moves. 'When will he come?' she says."

"Is it Kay you mean?" asked little Gerda.

"I tell only my own story, my own dream," the convolvulus answered.

What did the little snowdrop say?

"Between the trees a board hangs by two ropes; it's a swing. Two pretty little girls in snow-white dresses sit swinging; long green silk ribbons are fluttering from their hats. Their brother, who is bigger than they are, is standing up in the swing with his arm round the rope to keep himself steady, for in one hand he holds a little bowl and in the other a clay pipe; he is blowing soap bubbles. To and fro goes the swing, while the bubbles float away in a rainbow of changing colors; the last one still clings to the pipe and sways in the wind. The swing still moves, to and fro. The little black dog, as light as the bubbles, leaps up on his hind-legs; he wants to join the others on the swing. But it swoops past, out of reach, and the dog flops down, barking furiously. The children laugh; the bubbles burst. A swinging plank, a white flash of dissolving foam — that is my picture; that's my song."

"Your story may be beautiful, but you make it sound so sad, and you don't mention little Kay at all. Hyacinths, what have you to tell?"

"There were three lovely sisters, fragile, exquisite; one wore a dress of rose-red, the second of violet-blue, the third, pure white. Hand in hand they danced by the silent lake in the clear moonlight. They were not fairies, they were children of men. A sweet scent filled the air and the girls vanished into the wood. The fragrance grew more powerful; three coffins, in which lay three lovely girls, glided from the depths of the wood, over the lake; fireflies flew around them like tiny flickering lamps. Are the dancing maidens sleeping or are they dead? Perhaps, from the scent of the flowers, they are dead, and the bells are ringing for them."

"You make me feel dreadfully sad," said little Gerda. "And your own scent is so powerful that I can't help thinking of those sleeping girls. Can little Kay really be dead? The roses have been in the ground, and they say no."

"Ding dong!" rang out the hyacinth bells. "We're not ringing for little Kay; we don't know him. All we sing is our own song, the only one we know."

So Gerda went to the buttercup, which shone out from its fresh green leaves. "You are a bright little sun!" said Gerda. "Tell me if you know where I can find my playmate."

The buttercup shone very prettily, and looked up at Gerda. Now what song would the buttercup sing? Not one that gave her news of little Kay.

"In a small back yard the heavenly sun shone bright and warm; it was the first day of spring, and the sunbeams slid down the neighbor's whitewashed wall. Nearby, the first yellow flowers of spring were growing, gleaming just like gold in the golden rays. The old grandmother sat outside in her chair; her granddaughter, a poor servant girl, but pretty enough, had come home for a short visit, and now she kissed her grandmother. There was heart's gold in that kiss in the golden morning. That's all; there's my story."

"My poor old granny!" sighed Gerda. "I'm sure she's longing for me and grieving, just as she grieved about little Kay. But I'll soon be home again, and bring Kay with me. It's no use asking the flowers — their own tales are all they know, and they tell me nothing at all."

She tucked up her dress so that she could run fast, and away she went. Then something struck her leg quite smartly as she leapt over it; she looked — and it was a narcissus. "Maybe *you* have news for me," she thought, and she bent down towards the flower.

"I see myself! I see myself!" said the narcissus. "Ah, what a sweet perfume! High up in her attic lodging is a little ballet dancer. She stands on tiptoe, now on one leg, now on the other, and kicks out at the world. It is all in the mind, you know. Now she pours water from the kettle on to a piece of cloth — it's her dancer's bodice; cleanliness is next to godliness, as they say. Her white dress hangs on a peg; that too has been washed, then hung on the roof to dry. Now she puts it on, and round her neck she ties a saffron yellow scarf. It makes the dress seem even whiter. She raises one leg high in the air. How elegantly she stands and sways on her stalk! I see myself! I see myself!"

"That is your story, not mine," said Gerda. "I don't want to hear any more." She ran to the edge of the garden. The gate was locked, but she twisted the rusty fastening until it came away; the gate flew open and little Gerda ran out barefooted into the wide world. Three times she looked back, but nobody was following her. At last she could run no further, so she sat down on a big stone. As she gazed around her, she realized that summer was over; it was late autumn. There had been no signs of changing time in that enchanted garden, where the bright sun always shone, and flowers of every season bloomed together.

"Oh, I have lingered here too long," said little Gerda. "Autumn has come; I dare not stop!" She got up from the stone and started off once more. How tired and sore her feet were! How cold and damp was the countryside! The long willow leaves had turned quite yellow and wet with mist; they dropped off one by one. Only the thorny sloe had kept its fruit, but that was so sour that the thought of it twisted your mouth. Oh, how mournful and bleak it was in the wide world!

PART FOUR

Prince and Princess

Gerda soon had to rest again. And there, hopping about in the snow, right in front of her, was a raven. He had been staring at her for some time, with his head on one side, then on the other. Now he greeted her, "Caw, caw! How do, how do!" It may not have been an elegant way of speaking, but it was kindly meant. He asked her where she was going, all alone in the wide world. So she told the raven her story and asked if he had seen little Kay.

The raven nodded thoughtfully, and said, "Could be! Could be!"

"Oh — you really think that you have some news?" cried the little girl. And she hugged the bird so tightly that she nearly squeezed him to death.

"Caw, caw! Care-ful, care-ful!" the raven said. "I think that it may have been little Kay. But I fancy that by this time he will have forgotten you for the princess."

"Does he live with a princess?" asked Gerda.

"Now listen and I'll tell you," said the raven. "But I find it so hard to talk your language. If only you understood raven-speech I could tell you better."

"No, I never learned that," said Gerda, "though my granny knew it and other strange things too. I only wish I did."

"Well, never mind," said the raven. "I'll tell you as plainly as I can; you can't ask for more." And then he related what he knew. "In the kingdom where we are now, a princess dwells. She is extremely clever; she has read

all the newspapers in the world and has forgotten them again – that's how clever she is. She was sitting on her throne the other day when she happened to hear a little song. It goes like this: *Why should I not married be? Why not? Why not? Why not?* 'Well, there's something to be said for that,' she thought. So she decided to find a partner, but she wanted one who could speak for himself when spoken to — one who didn't just stand and look important. That's very dull. She ordered her ladies-in-waiting to be called together (it was done by sounding a roll of drums) — and when they heard her plan they were delighted. 'What a splendid idea!' 'We were thinking something of the kind just the other day!' They went on making remarks like these. All that I'm telling you is perfectly true," said the raven. "I've a tame sweetheart who has a free run of the palace, and I heard the tale from her."

Need I tell you that the sweetheart was also a raven? Birds will be birds, and a raven's mate is a raven.

"The newspapers promptly came out with a border of hearts and the princess's monogram. They announced that any good-looking young man might come to the palace and meet the princess; the one who seemed most at home in the princess's company but who was also the best and most interesting talker — that was the one she meant to choose.

"Well, the suitors flocked to the palace — there was never such a crowd! But nobody won the prize, either the first day, or the next. They could all talk smartly enough when they were out in the street, but when they came through the palace gate and saw the guards in their silver uniforms, and the footmen in gold all the way up the stairs, and the great halls with their brilliant lights — they seemed to be struck dumb. And when they stood before the throne where the princess sat, they could find nothing to say but the last word she had spoken herself, and she had no wish to hear *that* again. Though once they were back in the street, it was all chatter, chatter as before. There was a queue stretching away right from the city gate to the palace. I went over myself to have a look," said the raven.

"But Kay, little Kay!" asked Gerda. "When did he come? Was he in that crowd?"

"Give me time! Give me time! We're coming to him! It was on the third day when a little chap appeared without horse or carriage, and stepped jauntily up to the palace. His eyes were shining, just like yours, he had fine thick flowing hair — but his clothes, I must say, were shabby."

"That was Kay!" cried Gerda. "Oh, I have found him at last!" And she clapped her hands with joy.

"He had a little knapsack, or bundle, on his back," said the raven.

"Ah, that must have been his sledge," said Gerda. "He had it when he left."

"It may have been," said the raven. "I didn't study it all that closely. But I do know from my tame sweetheart that when he reached the palace gate and saw the guards in silver and the footmen in gold, he was not in the least bit dismayed. He only nodded pleasantly and said to them, 'It must be dull work standing there; I'd sooner go inside.'

"The great halls blazed with light; it was enough to make anyone feel small. The young chap's boots squeaked dreadfully, but even this didn't trouble him."

"That's certainly Kay!" cried Gerda. "His boots were new, I know; I heard them squeaking in my grandmother's kitchen."

"Well, they squeaked, to be sure," said the raven. "But he went merrily up to the princess, who was sitting on a pearl as big as a spinning wheel; all the ladies-in-waiting, with their maids, and their maids' maids, and all the gentlemen courtiers with their serving-men and their serving-men's serving-men were ranged around her in order."

"But did Kay win the princess?" asked little Gerda.

"If I hadn't been a bird I would have had a try myself, betrothed or not betrothed," the raven said. "He is said to have spoken as well as I do when I speak in my own raven language — or so my tame sweetheart tells me. He was so lively and confident; he hadn't come to woo the princess, he declared, only to hear her wise conversation. He liked it very well, and she liked him."

"Oh, that was certainly Kay," said Gerda. "He was so clever, he could do mental arithmetic, with fractions! Oh, do please take me to the palace."

"That's easily said," replied the raven, "but how is it to be done? I must talk to my tame sweetheart about it; she'll be able to advise us, I have no doubt, for — let me tell you — a girl like you would never be allowed to enter in the regular way."

"Oh, I shall get in," said Gerda. "When Kay knows I am here he'll come straight out and fetch me."

"Well," said the raven, waggling his head, "wait for me by the stile." And off he flew.

It was late in the evening when he returned. "Ra-a-ax! Ra-a-ax!" he cawed. "I'm to give you my sweetheart's greetings, and here's a piece of bread from the kitchen; there's plenty there, and you must be hungry. It's impossible for you to get into the palace as you are, without even shoes on your feet; but don't cry. My sweetheart knows a little back staircase that leads to the royal bedroom, and she knows where to find the key!"

So they went into the garden, and along the avenue where the leaves were falling, leaf after leaf; then, when all the lights in the palace had gone out, one by one, the raven led little Gerda to a small back door.

Oh, how Gerda's heart beat with hope and fear! It was just as if she were about to do something wrong — yet all she wanted was to find out if the boy really was little Kay. Oh yes, he must be Kay; she could see him in her mind so vividly with his bright clever eyes and smooth flowing hair; she remembered the way he used to smile when they sat together at home among the roses. Oh, he would surely be glad to see her, to hear what a long way she had come for his sake, and to know how grieved they had all been at home when he never returned. She trembled with fear, and hope.

They had now reached the staircase where the tame raven was waiting; a little lamp was glimmering on a stand. Gerda curtseyed, as her grand-mother had taught her.

"My fiancé has spoken most charmingly of you, my dear young lady," said the tame raven, "and your life-history, as we may call it, really touches the heart. If you will kindly take the lamp, I will lead the way. Straight on is best and shortest — we are not likely to meet anyone."

"Yet I can't help feeling that someone is following behind," said Gerda. And indeed, something did seem to rush along past her; it looked like a flight of shadows on the wall, horses with thin legs and flowing manes, huntsmen, lords and ladies on horseback.

"Those are only dreams," said the tame raven. "They come and take the gentry's thoughts on midnight rides and that's a good thing, for you will be able to observe them more safely while they are asleep. But I hope that you will show a thankful heart if you do rise to fame and fortune."

"Now, now, there's no need to talk about that," said the woodland raven.

They entered the first room, where the walls were hung with rose-colored satin embroidered with flowers. Here, the dreams were racing past so swiftly that Gerda could not distinguish any one of the lords and ladies. Each hall that she passed through was more magnificent than the one before; then, at last, they arrived at the royal bedroom.

The ceiling was like the crown of a palm tree, with leaves of rarest crystal; and, hanging from a thick gold stem in the centre of the floor, were two beds, each in the shape of a lily. One was white, and in this lay the princess. The other was scarlet — and in this Gerda knew that she must look for little Kay. She turned one of the red leaves over, and saw a boy's brown hair. It was Kay! She cried his name aloud, holding the lamp near his face; the dreams on their wild steeds came whirling back to the sleeper; he woke — he turned his head — it was not little Kay.

No, it was not little Kay, though the prince too was a handsome boy. And now the princess looked out from the white lily bed and asked what was happening. Little Gerda wept as she told her story, but she did not forget to speak of the ravens and their kind help.

"You poor child," said the prince and princess, and they praised the

ravens, adding, though, that they must not do it again. This time, all things considered, they would be given a reward.

"Would you like to fly away free?" the princess asked. "Or would you like a permanent place as Court Ravens, with all the odds and ends you want from the kitchens?"

Both the ravens bowed and prudently chose the permanent place, for they had to think of their old age. "It's a good thing to have something by for a rainy day," they said. The prince stepped out of his bed so that Gerda could sleep in it — and who could do more than that? As Gerda slept, the dreams came flying back — but this time they looked like angels; they seemed to be drawing a sledge, on which Kay was sitting, nodding at her. But this was only a dream, and it vanished as soon as she woke.

The next day she was dressed from top to toe in silk and velvet. She was invited to stay at the palace and pass delightful days, but she begged to have just a little carriage with a horse to draw it, and a pair of boots small enough for her feet; with these she could drive out into the wide world and seek for little Kay.

She was given not only boots but a muff, and when she was ready to leave, in beautiful fine warm clothes, a new carriage of pure gold drew up before the door; on it the coat-of-arms of the royal pair glistened like a star. Coachman, footmen and outriders — for there were outriders too — all wore gold crowns. The prince and princess personally helped her into the carriage and wished her good luck. The forest raven, who had now married his sweetheart, came along for the first twelve miles or so; he sat beside her, for he could not bear travelling backwards. The tame bird stood in the gateway flapping her wings; she didn't go with them because too much rich palace fare had given her a headache. The inside of the coach was lined with iced cake and sugar candy, while the space beneath the seat was packed with fruit and ginger nuts.

"Farewell! Farewell!" cried the prince and princess, and little Gerda wept. So did the raven, and in this way they passed the first few miles. Then the raven said his own goodbye, and that was the hardest parting of them all. He flew up into a tree and flapped his black wings as long as he could see the carriage, which gleamed as bright as the sun.

PART FIVE

The Little Robber Girl

They drove through the dark forest, but the carriage shone like a fiery torch; it dazzled the eyes of the robber band – they could not bear it.

"It's gold! It's gold!" they roared. Then, rushing forward, they seized the horses, killed the outriders, coachman, and footmen, and dragged little Gerda out of the carriage.

"She's plump; she's a dainty dish; she's been fed on nut kernels!" said the old robber woman, who had a long bristly beard and shaggy eyebrows hanging over her eyes. "She's as tender and sweet as a little fat lamb. Yum, yum! She'll make a tasty dinner!" She drew out a bright sharp knife, which glittered quite dreadfully.

"Ouch!" screeched the hag all at once. She had been bitten in the ear by her own little daughter who hung on her back, and who was so wild and mischievous that she was quite out of hand. "You loathsome brat!" said her mother, and forgot what she had meant to do with Gerda.

"She shall be my playmate," said the little robber girl. "She shall give me her muff and pretty clothes and sleep with me in my bed." And so spoilt and wilful was she that of course she had her own way. She got in the coach with Gerda, and away they drove, through bush and briar, deeper and deeper into the forest. The little girl was no taller than Gerda, but much sturdier, with broader shoulders and darker skin. Her eyes were quite black, with a curious look of melancholy in them. She put her arm round little Gerda and said, "They shan't kill you – not as long as I don't get cross with you. You're a princess, I suppose?"

"No," said Gerda, and again she told all her adventures, and how fond she was of little Kay.

The robber girl watched her seriously, and nodded her head. "They shan't kill you even if I do get cross with you," she said. "I'll do it myself." Then she dried Gerda's eyes and put both her hands into the pretty muff which was so soft and warm.

Suddenly the carriage stopped; they had reached the courtyard of the robbers' castle. Its walls were cracked from top to bottom; crows and ravens were flying out of the gaps and holes, while huge hounds, each one looking as if he could swallow a man, leapt high into the air; but not a single bark came from them, for that was forbidden. In the great old hall, cobwebbed and black with soot, a large fire burned on the stone floor; the smoke drifted about under the roof, trying to find its own way out. A vast cauldron of soup was bubbling away; hares and rabbits were roasting on turning-spits.

"Tonight you shall sleep with me and all my pets," said the robber girl. First they had something to eat and drink, then they went over to a corner where straw and blankets were scattered. Above them in holes and on ledges about a hundred pigeons were roosting; they seemed asleep but a slight stir ran through them when the little girls appeared.

"They're mine – all of them," said the little robber girl. She seized one of the nearest, took it by the legs and shook it until it flapped its wings. "Kiss it!" she cried, waving it in Gerda's face. Then she pointed to some wooden bars nailed over a hole above their heads. "Those are woodland riff-raff, both of them. They'd fly off in a flash if they weren't locked up. And here's my special sweetheart, Bae." She pulled a reindeer forward by the horn; it was tethered to the wall, with a shiny copper ring round its neck. "He's another one who'd fly off if we didn't keep him prisoner. Every night I tickle his neck with my sharp knife – he doesn't care for that!" And drawing a long knife out of a crack in the wall, she ran it lightly across the reindeer's neck. The poor creature struggled and kicked, but the robber girl laughed, and pulled Gerda down with her under the rug.

"Are you taking that knife into bed with you?" Gerda asked, as she looked at it nervously.

"I always sleep with a knife at hand," said the little robber girl. "You never know what may happen. But now tell me again about little Kay and why you came out into the wide world." So Gerda told her tale once more, from the very beginning, and the wood-pigeons moaned in the cage, and the other pigeons slept. Then the little robber girl fell asleep too, one arm round Gerda's neck, the other holding the knife; you could hear that she slept from her breathing. But Gerda couldn't even close her eyes, not knowing whether she was to live or die. The robbers sat round the fire and drank and sang, and the robber woman turned somersaults. It was a frightful sight to behold.

Then all at once the wood-pigeons cried, "Rr-coo! Mm-coo! We have seen little Kay! A white hen was carrying his sledge, and he was sitting in the Snow Queen's carriage which swept low over the forest where we lay in the nest. She breathed down on us young ones and all except the two of us here froze to death. Rr-coo! Mm-coo!"

"What are you saying up there?" cried Gerda. "Which way did the Snow Queen go? Can you tell me?"

"She must have been making for Lapland, for you'll always find snow and ice there. You ask the reindeer; he's sure to know."

"Yes, it's a land of ice and snow; everything there is lovely and pleasant," the reindeer said. "You can run and leap to your heart's delight in the great shining valleys. There the Snow Queen has her summer palace, but her real home is in a castle far off towards the North Pole, on an island called Spitzbergen."

"Oh, Kay, poor Kay!" sighed Gerda.

"Lie still, you," said the robber girl, "or you'll get my knife in your middle!"

When morning came, Gerda told her all that the wood-pigeons had said. The little robber girl looked very grave, but she nodded and said, "Never mind — never mind; it's all one … Do you know where Lapland is?" she asked the reindeer.

"Who should know better than I?" said the reindeer, and his eyes shone at the thought of it. "I was born and bred in that land; once I could leap and play freely there in the snowfields."

"Listen to me," said the robber girl to Gerda. "All our menfolk are out. My old ma's still here and here she'll stay — but later in the morning she'll take a swig from that big bottle and after that she'll have forty winks. Then I'll see what I can do for you." She jumped out of bed, ran across to her mother, pulled her by the beard and called, "Good morning, my dear old nanny-goat!" Her mother flipped her on the nose making it quite red and blue – but it was all for sheer affection.

Then, when her mother had had a drink from the bottle and was taking a nap, the robber girl went over to the reindeer. "I'd love to go on teasing you a few more times with that sharp knife of mine because you always look so funny when I do – but never mind, I'm going to set you free so that you can run to Lapland. But you must put your best foot foremost and take this little girl for me to the Snow Queen's palace, where her playmate is. I expect you've heard her story; she was talking loudly enough, and you are always one for eavesdropping."

The reindeer leapt for joy. The robber girl lifted Gerda on to his back, taking care to tie her firmly on, with a little cushion for a seat.

"You'll be all right," she said. "Here are your fur boots – you'll need them in that cold – but I shall keep your muff; it's far too pretty to lose. Still, you won't have to freeze; here are my mother's big gloves. They reach right up to your elbows. Shove your hands in! Now they look just like my ugly old mother's!"

Gerda wept with happiness.

"I can't stand that snivelling," said the little robber girl. "You ought to be looking really pleased. Here are two loaves and a ham, so you won't starve." These provisions were tied to the reindeer's back. Then the little robber girl opened the door and called in all the big dogs; after that she cut the rope with her knife and said to the reindeer, "Off you go! But take good care of the little girl!"

Gerda stretched out her hands in the enormous gloves and called "Goodbye!" to the robber girl, and the reindeer sped away past bush and briar, through the great forest, over marsh and moor, and the wide plains, as swiftly as he could go. The wolves howled; the ravens screamed; the sky seemed filled with sneezing, crackling noises – schooo, schooo; piff, piff – each time with a glow of red. "Those are my dear old Northern

Lights," said the reindeer. "Aren't they beautiful!" Faster and faster he ran, through the night, through the day. The loaves were finished, and the ham — then they were in Lapland.

PART SIX

The Lapland Woman and the Finmark Woman

They stopped at a little hut, a wretched place; the roof nearly touched the ground and the door was so low that the family had to get down on all fours to crawl in and out. Nobody was at home except an old Lapp woman, who was frying fish over an oil lamp. The reindeer told her Gerda's story, but first it told its own, which seemed the more important. Gerda was too frozen with cold to speak at all.

"Oh, you poor things!" cried the Lapland woman. "You've a long way to go yet. You still have several hundred miles to cross before you get to Finmark — that's where the Snow Queen is just now, sending off those fireworks of hers every night. I'll write you a few words on a piece of dried codfish — I've got no paper — and you take it to the Finnwoman living up there. She can tell you better than I can what to do." And so, when Gerda was properly warm and had had some supper, the Lapland woman wrote some words on a piece of dried cod and told Gerda to take good care of it. Then she fastened her on the reindeer's back again, and off they sped. "Schooo, schooo! Crack! Crack!" came the noises from the sky, and all night long the glorious Northern Lights flashed violet-blue. At last they arrived in Finmark and knocked on the Finnwoman's chimney, for she hadn't even a door.

Inside, it was so swelteringly hot that the Finnwoman wore hardly a stitch of clothing. She was small and dumpy, with a brownish skin. The first thing she did was to loosen little Gerda's clothes, and take off her boots and thick gloves; then she laid a piece of ice on the reindeer's head; then studied what was written on the dried-fish letter. She read it three

times; after that she knew it by heart, and she dropped it into the cooking pot, for she never wasted anything.

The reindeer now told his story, and after that, little Gerda's; and the Finnwoman's wise eyes twinkled, but she didn't say a word.

"Ah, you're so clever," said the reindeer. "I know you can tie up all the winds in the world with a single thread; when the captain undoes the first knot he gets a fair wind; if he undoes the second, then gusts begin to blow; if he undoes the third and fourth, a gale roars up that hurls down the forest trees and wrecks the ship. Won't you make this little girl a magic drink that will give her the strength of twelve men, so that she can overcome the Snow Queen?"

"The strength of twelve men?" said the Finmark woman. "A lot of good *that* would be!" She went over to a shelf and took down a rolled-up parchment. She opened it out; strange letters were written on it, and she read so intently that the sweat ran from her brow like rain.

But the reindeer went on pleading so hard for little Gerda, and Gerda looked at her with such tearful beseeching eyes, that once again she turned her gaze on them. Then, drawing the reindeer into a corner, she put fresh ice on his head and whispered in his ear: "Little Kay is with the Snow Queen, sure enough; he finds everything there to his liking, and thinks that he's in the finest place in the world — but all that is because he has a splinter of glass in his heart, and another in his eye. These must come out or he'll stay bewitched, and the Snow Queen will keep her hold over him for ever!"

"But is there nothing that you can give little Gerda to break that hold?"

"I cannot give her greater power than she has already. Don't you see how great that is? How men and beasts all feel that they must serve her? How far she has come in the wide world on her own bare feet? She must not learn of her power; it comes from her own heart, from her being a dear and innocent child. If she can't find her own way into the Snow Queen's palace and free little Kay, there is nothing that we can do to help. Now! About ten miles further north is the edge of the Snow Queen's garden. You can carry the little girl as far as that, then put her down by the big bush with red berries, standing in the snow; don't stay gossiping, but hurry back here." With that, the Finnwoman lifted little Gerda on to the reindeer's back, and off he dashed as fast as his legs could go.

"Oh! I've left my boots behind! And my gloves!" cried little Gerda. She felt stung by the piercing cold. But the reindeer dared not stop; on he ran till he came to the big bush with the red berries. There he put Gerda down, and kissed her on the lips; as he did so, great shining tears ran down the poor animal's face. Then he turned and sped back as fast as he was able.

And there was poor Gerda, without boots, without gloves, in the midst of that terrible icy land and its piercing cold.

She started to run forward, but a whole regiment of snowflakes appeared in front of her. They had not fallen from above, for the sky was quite clear, sparkling with Northern Lights. These flakes came running along the ground, and the nearer they came the larger they grew. Gerda remembered how strange and wonderfully made the flakes had seemed when she'd looked at them through the magnifying glass. How long ago that was. But these were far bigger and much more frightening — they were the Snow Queen's frontier guards. They had the weirdest, most fantastic shapes. Some were like huge wild hedgehogs; others were like knotted bunches of snakes writhing their heads in all directions; others again were like fat little bears with icicles for hair. All of them were glistening white; all were living snowflakes.

Then little Gerda began to say the Lord's Prayer, and the cold was so intense that she could see her own breath; it rose from her mouth like a cloud. The cloud became thicker and thicker, and took the form of little bright angels who grew in size the moment they touched the ground. On their heads were helmets; in their hands were spears and shields. By the time Gerda had finished her prayer, she was encircled by a whole legion of these spirits. They struck out at the dreadful snow-things, shattering them into hundreds of pieces, and Gerda was able to go on her way without fear or danger. The angels patted her feet and hands so that she hardly felt the biting cold, and she hurried on towards the Snow Queen's palace.

But now we must see how little Kay was faring. Whatever his thoughts, they were not of Gerda; he certainly did not dream that she was just outside the palace.

PART SEVEN
What Happened at the Snow Queen's Palace and What Took Place After That

The palace walls were of driven snow, and the doors and windows of cutting wind. There were over a hundred halls, just as the drifting snow had formed them; the largest stretched for miles. All were lit by the brilliant Northern Lights; they were vast, empty, glittering, bleak as ice and deathly cold. In the very midst of the palace there was a frozen lake; it had split into a thousand pieces, but each piece was exactly like the next so that it seemed not an accident but a cunning work of art. The Snow Queen always sat in the centre of this lake whenever she was at home; she used to say that she was on the Mirror of Reason, the best — indeed, the only glass that mattered — in the world.

Little Kay was quite blue with cold; in fact, he was nearly black. But he never noticed, for the Snow Queen had kissed away his shivering and his heart was hardly more than a lump of ice. He was busily dragging about some sharp flat pieces of ice, arranging them in every possible pattern. What he was trying to do was to make a special word, and this he could never manage, try as he would. The word was ETERNITY. For the Snow Queen had said to him, "If you can spell out *that* for me, you shall be your own master, and I'll make you a present of the whole world,

together with a new pair of skates." But he still could not manage it.

"Now I must fly off to the warm lands," said the Snow Queen. "I want to take a peep into the black cauldrons." (She meant the volcanoes, Etna and Vesuvius.) "I shall whiten their tops a little; it does them good after all those lemons and grapes." Off she flew, and Kay was left quite alone in the vast empty hall, gazing at the pieces of ice, and thinking, thinking, until his head seemed to crack. There he sat, stiff and still; anyone might have thought that he was frozen to death.

It was just then that little Gerda stepped into the palace through the great doors of cutting winds. But she said her evening prayer, and the cold winds dropped as if they were falling asleep. She entered the vast cold empty hall – and there was Kay! She knew him at once; she rushed towards him and flung her arms about his neck crying, "Kay! Dear little Kay! I've found you at last!" But he sat there quite still, stiff and cold.

Then Gerda began to weep hot tears; they fell on his breast and reached right through to his heart. There, they thawed the lump of ice, and washed away the splinter of glass. Kay looked up at her, and she sang the verse that they used to sing together.

> *"In the vale the rose grows wild;*
> *Children play all the day —*
> *One of them is the Christ-child."*

Then tears came into Kay's eyes too. And, as he cried, the second splinter of glass was washed away; now he could recognize her, and he cried out joyfully: "Gerda! Dear little Gerda! Where have you been all this time? And what has been happening to me?" He looked around him. "How cold it is! How huge and empty!" The air was so filled with their happiness that even the pieces of ice began dancing for sheer delight, and when they were tired and lay down again they formed the very word which the Snow Queen had told Kay to make — the one for which he would be his own master, and be given the whole world, and a new pair of skates.

Then Gerda kissed his cheeks, and their colour came back to them; she kissed his eyes, and they shone like hers; she kissed his hands and feet, and he was well and sound, and warm, the Kay she had always known. The Snow Queen could now come back as soon as she liked; Kay's sign of release was there, laid out in shining letters of ice.

Hand in hand, they walked out of the great echoing palace. Wherever they went the winds were still and the sun broke out. When they reached the bush with the red berries, there stood the reindeer, waiting for them. With him was a young doe, and she gave warm milk to the boy and girl. Then the reindeer and the doe carried Kay and Gerda first to the Finmark woman, where they warmed themselves in the hot room and were given advice about the journey home — and then to the Lapland woman. She had made new clothes for them, and had prepared a sledge.

The reindeer and the doe bounded along right up to the borders of

the country. There, Kay and Gerda could see the first green shoots of spring coming out of the ground; the sledge could go no further, and the reindeer and the Lapland woman had to return to the north. "Farewell! Farewell! Goodbye! Goodbye!" said each and all.

The first little birds of spring began to twitter; the first green leaves appeared on the forest trees, and through the wood came a young girl riding a splendid horse. Gerda knew that horse, for it had been harnessed to her golden coach. The young girl had a scarlet cap on her head and pistols at her side. She was the robber girl! She was tired of home life, she told them, and was making for the north; if she did not like it there she would try some other direction. She recognized Gerda at once and Gerda recognized her; they were both delighted to meet each other again.

"You're a fine one to go straying off like that!" she said to Kay. "I wonder if you deserve to have anyone running to the ends of the earth for your sake!"

But Gerda patted her cheek and asked after the prince and princess.

"They've gone travelling to foreign parts," said the robber girl.

"And the raven?"

"Oh, the raven's dead," she replied. "His tame sweetheart's a widow now and wears a piece of black wool on her leg. She's always moaning and groaning but it doesn't mean a thing. Now you tell me your adventures, and how you managed to find him." And Gerda and Kay both told their separate tales.

"Well, well, well; today's mishap is tomorrow's story," said the robber girl. She took each of them by the hand, and promised that if she ever passed through their town she would pay them a visit. Then she rode away, into the wide world.

But Kay and Gerda went on, hand in hand. As they went, the spring flowered round them, beautiful with blossoms and green leaves. They heard the church bells ringing; they saw ahead the towers and walls of a city; they were nearing home.

And they entered the town, and went up the stairs of the grandmother's house, and into the room near the roof, where everything stood just where it was before, and the clock still said "Tick-tock", and the hands still marked the hours. But as they went through the door they noticed that they themselves had grown; they were not young children. The roses in the wooden boxes were flowering at the open window, and out there were their own little wooden stools. Kay and Gerda sat down on them and held each other's hands. The terrible icy splendor of the Snow Queen's palace had slipped away from their minds like a distant dream. Grandmother sat beside them in the heavenly sunshine and read to them from the Bible. "Except ye become as little children, ye shall not enter into the Kingdom of Heaven."

Kay and Gerda looked into each other's eyes, and at once they remembered the old song, and saw its meaning:

"*In the vale the rose grows wild;*
Children play all the day —
One of them is the Christ-child."

So there they sat together, the same children still at heart. And it was summer, warm delightful summer ...

Acknowledgments

Every effort has been made to credit the material reproduced in this book. The publisher apologizes if inadvertently any source remains unacknowledged.

Goldilocks and the Three Bears text from *English Fairy Tales* © The Hamlyn Publishing Group Ltd 1965, used with permission of Egmont Children's Books Limited © illustrations Wendy Smith 1999

Henny-Penny text by Joseph Jacobs, amended and updated © illustrations Nicholas Allan 1999

The Three Little Pigs © illustrations Rob Lewis 1999

The Emperor's New Clothes published by Hutchinson Children's Books and Atlantic Monthly Press – Little Brown © text and illustrations Nadine Bernard Westcott

Red Riding Hood used by permission of Dial Books for Young Readers, a division of Penguin Putnam Inc. and the Sheldon Fogelman Agency Inc. © text and illustrations James Marshall 1987

Jack and the Beanstalk used by permission of Oxford University Press © text and illustrations Val Biro 1987

The Elves and the Shoemaker © Nord-Süd Verlag AG, Gossau Zurich 1986

Cinderella published by The Bodley Head © text Kathleen Lines 1970 © illustrations Shirley Hughes 1970

The Selfish Giant published by Hutchinson Children's Books, used by permission of Bohem Press, Zurich © text and illustrations Allison Reed 1983

Puss in Boots published in a fully illustrated edition by Andersen Press © text and illustrations Tony Ross 1981

The Sorcerer's Apprentice from *Stuff and Nonsense* published by The Bodley Head © text Laura Cecil 1989 © illustrations Emma Chichester Clark 1989

The Ugly Duckling text from *The Complete Fairy Tales and Stories of Hans Andersen* published by Victor Gollancz/ Hamish Hamilton © text translation Erik Haugaard 1974 © illustrations Alison Catley 1999

The Twelve Dancing Princesses published by Faber & Faber © text Faber & Faber 1978 © illustrations Errol Le Cain 1978

The Sleeping Beauty © illustrations Jan Pancheri 1999

Hansel and Gretel from *Grimms' Fairy Tales* published by Hutchinson Children's Books © text Hutchinson Children's Books 1985 © illustrations Lemniscaat Publishers, Rotterdam 1985

Compiled and
edited by Madeleine Nicklin

Designed by Paul Welti
Typesetting by Peter Howard

First published in the United Kingdom in 1999 by
Hutchinson Children's Books
Random House UK Limited

This edition published by Barnes & Noble, Inc.,
by arrangement with Random House Children's Books UK

1999 Barnes & Noble Books

ISBN 0-7607-1791-5

Printed and bound in Singapore

99 00 01 02 03 04 MC 9 8 7 6 5 4 3 2

Tien Wah Press [Pte] Ltd